"Name your price and let's have done with the farce, girl."

"I am not 'your girl' and I have no intention of being, you pompous beast," Jena snapped.

"I may have been drunk as a lord last night, my dear," Dev ground out, "but I am not a wet-behind-the-ears nodcock eager to be taken in by some wide-eyed, soft-spoken Cyprian."

"How dare you, sirrah!"

Jena leaped to her feet, fury blinding her to her own actions. She raised the vase over her head and deliberately smashed it in the very center of the desk. Her whole body trembled in reaction to her outrageous behavior.

"I'm terribly sorry that I lost my temper," Jena apologized.

Dev liked the slight musical tone of her low voice and was impressed with the air of quality that pervaded the girl's behavior. Once they reached an agreement he was more than ever convinced she would make an exciting lover. . . .

Also by Martha Jean Powers
Published by Fawcett Crest Books:

PROXY BRIDE

GAZEBO RENDEZVOUS

THE GRAY
FOX
WAGERS

Martha Jean Powers

FAWCETT CREST • NEW YORK

To
Hazel F. Powers
Who, despite my sneakers,
always made me feel welcome.

A Fawcett Crest Book
Published by Ballantine Books
Copyright © 1988 by Martha Jean Powers

Library of Congress Catalog Card Number: 88-91116

ISBN 0-449-21465-6

Manufactured in the United States of America

First Edition: October 1988

Chapter One

"Come on, luv. Help me off with this dress."

Jena's slender hands fumbled with the buttons on the back of Lucy's dress and she cursed her own embarrassment at the voluptuous blond woman's nudity. After three months she ought to be used to the casual immodesty of the actresses in the dressing room. The last button was pushed through the loop and Lucy's bosom burst free of the nest of pink netting which made up the skimpy bodice. Casually the woman stepped out of the dress and tossed it to the red-faced seamstress.

"Thanks, dearie," Lucy said. She made no attempt to cover herself as she strutted to the long, mirrored dressing tables, chatting easily with the other women in various stages of undress. "The boys in the pit are in rare form tonight. I sang a chorus too close to the edge and one of them tried to grab my bleedin' foot. Right saucy little bugger, he was."

Jena shook out the pink dress, looking it over carefully for any rips or torn seams. As her fingers found a jagged tear in the skirt, she wrinkled her nose in annoyance. She tried not to listen to the lively conversation among the women. As usual, they were absorbed in itemizing the physical and financial attributes of the men in the audience. When Jena first came to work at the theater, the women had delighted in her shocked expression and had tried to outdo each other in scandalizing the young innocent. They were all too aware that Jena was an outsider, from her softly enunciated words to her air of modest propriety. Thankfully, the novelty of Jena's presence had worn off now, and for the most part they ignored her.

Wearily she folded the pink dress over her arm and then walked down the line of six chairs, picking up articles of clothing strewn on the floor. At the end of the dressing table, the room widened to accommodate the racks of costumes needed by the actresses. Surrounded by the colorful array of materials, Nanny Ginthner sat enthroned in a scarred rocking chair. The plump little woman was enveloped in a blue smock similar to the ones she wore in Jena's nursery days. From under the edge of her lace-trimmed mobcap, one white curl corkscrewed out and dangled saucily against her wrinkled cheek. Jena's gray eyes kindled with warmth and she hesitated, thinking the old woman was asleep. She tiptoed forward when Nanny's lids raised, spearing the young girl where she stood.

"No need to catfoot around, Miss Jena. I wasna sleepin'. Can't a body shut her eyes for a minute?" The sharp words were softened by the twinkle in her brown eyes.

"Even with your eyes closed you know what I'm up to," Jena said in chagrin. "You never missed anything that went on at Dunton House, Nanny."

A vision of Jena's family home rose unbidden at her words and the old woman pursed her lips, her face grim with memories. The young girl sighed, knowing how much her life had changed since the death of her father. Then Jena straightened her

2

shoulders, angry with herself for sliding back into the past. This garish room, the gaudy costumes, and the blowsy, overly made-up women were the present. Dunton House and her life as the pampered daughter of Sir George Christie would never return. It was up to her to make a new life.

"Sit down, child," Nanny said anxiously. "You're looking plumb peaky tonight."

Jena wiped a hand across her forehead, brushing a stray black curl behind her ear. She sat down on the stool poised beside the rocker and automatically reached into the sewing box on the low table in front of her. Extracting a needle and a spool of thread, she smiled at the old woman whose wan face reflected her own tiredness. As she threaded her needle, Jena watched the gnarled hands take tiny stitches in the patchwork skirt and was comforted by the familiar rhythm. She was unaware that the actresses had left the room until the unaccustomed silence broke in upon her thoughts.

"Just another hour, Nanny. Then we can go home," Jena announced, forcing her voice to sound more cheerful than relieved.

"Home, hah! A wee squalid room on a dirty side street!" Nanny spat the words out bitterly. "It's a sorry day when Lady Jena Christie should call the likes of that place home. Want of money, want of comfort."

In times of stress, Nanny quoted proverbs. When Jena was growing up she had enjoyed searching for the meaning behind each solemnly spoken adage. This time she had to agree that the dingy little room in a working-class section of town could hardly be termed comfortable. But they had very few options.

"Now, Nanny. Don't go getting yourself all in a pother. We've neither the money nor the connections to turn down Mistress McGuire's boarding-house. Who'd ever have thought London would be so expensive."

The old woman shook her head from side to side, clucking her tongue to indicate her own amazement. Her blue-veined hands rested quietly atop the patchwork skirt she was mending, and her rheumy eyes searched Jena's quietly sewing figure. From the moment that the tiny, squalling babe had been placed in her arms, Nanny had adored her little mistress. Jena's father, Sir George Christie, had doted on the child, never blaming her for her mother's death of childbed fever as many another man might. But it was Nanny who took on the day-to-day loving of the child, watching over her with the same fierce protection as a natural mother. And her babe had grown into a lovely girl, the old woman thought for the hundredth time.

Tendrils of black hair had worked loose from the heavy braid that hung down Jena's back. The wispy curls lay against her neck, in sharp contrast to the rosy tint of her flawless skin. Her flaring brows were bunched over her eyes as she concentrated on her stitches. Sadly, Nanny noted the girl's hands were no longer soft and delicate as befitted a society lady. Jena was now a member of the working class. Sensibly dressed in a brown high-necked merino wool dress, devoid of ruffles or trim. Well-worn, short boots peeked out from beneath the hem of her skirt.

Despite the soberness of her dress, there was a glow that surrounded Jena which had far more to do with her temperament than with her beauty. She had accepted her situation with a willing practicality, refusing to dwell on what might have been. Nanny, more than Jena, viewed the present with bitterness.

"It fair breaks my heart to look at you, Miss Jena. You should be wearing fancy gowns and out walking with suitors, instead of rubbing shoulders with the likes of those women." Nanny waved her hand in the direction of the stage, her mouth set in condemnation of the actresses.

"They've been kind enough," Jena said pacifically, bending her head over the rip she was sewing.

"No better than they should be, the lot of them," Nanny snorted. "Your father should see the fine mess you're in. Gambling away your very inheritance, hah!"

"Please, Nanny." Jena rapidly blinked the tears away as she thought of Sir George, her profligate father. She had loved him dearly and, despite her near destitute state, could never think of him without smiling. In the stables at home, Jena had tagged after her father, listening to his stories about each of the horses. She had gone to the racetracks with him and watched in fascination as he mingled comfortably with noblemen and their servants. Strangely enough, her father was more at home in the company of the trainers and grooms, since he believed these were the people who knew the actual worth of the horses. Sir George had an expansive charm and generous heart, but his weakness was gambling. When he won, he shared with his friends, especially those down on their luck. Unfortunately, he did not win as often as he lost. In the end he died as he had lived, surrounded by friends commiserating over the loss of a race.

"Ah, Miss Jena, if only you'd been able to stay on at Dunton House," Nanny said, leaning her head on the back of the rocker.

As always when she thought of her home and the breeding farm, a hard knot of anguish formed in

5

Jena's breast. Her father's debts had been far worse than she ever suspected. In order to pay off the creditors, the horses had to be sold. She had watched dry-eyed as each one was taken out of the stables, but her heart bled as though a part of her life was being torn away.

"There was no use in staying. With no income from the farm, we'd have starved along with the servants. By leasing the house, the servants were kept on and we have some money for necessities," Jena explained once more.

She thought of all the people who had worked for her family for generations. Even now they depended on her, and at times Jena felt weighted down by the responsibility. Leasing Dunton House was only a stopgap measure. She tried not to panic as she thought of the carefully hoarded gold pieces that dwindled each day. But the servants were her friends, and when a crisis arose, she felt she must offer what help she could. Jena had already used most of this month's allotment. Finding work in London had been far more difficult than she imagined. It had taken a month to find this position, and then the wages paid had really been for Nanny's skills, not Jena's.

For the most part, Jena had been raised to take up her predestined role in society. She had been taught to run a large establishment, learning to deal with the servants at an early age. Of prime importance, she was instructed in the social graces as befitted her rank. However, since her father supervised her development, there were considerable lapses and leeway given to her education. She was given more freedom than most girls her age. She had never learned to sketch or to do proper needlework. Talent and patience were needed for both, and Jena knew in these instances she had neither.

She had learned to play a guitar instead of a piano so that she could take her music with her when she roamed the estate.

Jena had enjoyed an unusual friendship with her father. He believed that she would one day take over the running of the stud farm, so he prepared her as he would a son. He brought in tutors to teach her subjects normally forbidden to females. Geography, philosophy, and science were added to her curriculum. He himself took on the task of educating her in the management of the farm. Unfortunately, with his untimely death, Jena's major accomplishment, running a stud farm, became useless.

Arriving in London with high hopes of employment, Jena discovered the brutal realities of life. For all her other education, Jena discovered that her social and domestic accomplishments were not in demand. Because of her background there were certain avenues of employment that were closed to her either out of pride, propriety, or ineptitude. Her diction and accent marked her as too high-toned to be hired as a servant. She had neither references nor skill enough to apply as a governess or a shop assistant. And her moral code prohibited her from accepting several generous propositions which had been extended. When the job as theater seamstress was offered, she accepted with alacrity. But Jena felt nearly desperate when she saw her money supply disappearing faster than she could replenish it.

"Don't worry, lamby," Nanny said as she patted the young girl's hands. "After a typhoon there are pears to gather. Sumthing will turn up."

As though the old woman had conjured up the devil, the door to the hallway opened and Jason Winestable peered around the edge. Seeing the two women, his bulbous eyes blinked and he straightened, throwing the door wide as he entered. Jena tried not to shrink before his lecherous glance, edging her stool closer to the rocking chair. Even in her fear she marveled that the enormously fat man could walk so silently across the wooden floor.

"Miss Christie. Nanny." Winestable's voice boomed around the dressing room and his heavy-lidded eyes shifted between the women, finally settling on the younger of the two. "Just wanted to pop in and see if you've reconsidered me offer. Rehearsals be starting next week, dearie."

Jena drew herself up at the oily manner of the middle-aged man, but his words sent her heart racing and she found she was having difficulty breathing. She was not exactly afraid of Mr. Winestable, but whenever she was near him she dreaded the possibility that he might touch her. She had noticed his hands when she first met him and had disliked the too white, too soft fingers that extended from the fleshy palms. If he touched her she would surely scream.

"I've explained before, Mr. Winestable, that Miss Christie cannot appear on your stage." Nanny's voice shook with outrage.

Yet for all her bravely spoken words, there was an air of fear about the old woman that made Jena wince. Poverty left little room for pride, Jena thought sadly, borrowing one of Nanny's proverbs.

"I'd prefer 'earing the words from the lady 'erself." Winestable's voice was affable, but there was a hint of steel behind the humor. "I've told you afore that I've a nice little part for you. Wouldn't 'ave to do much and you'd be a favorite of the young bucks in the pit."

Although Jena trembled at the audacious glitter in the man's eyes, she kept her expression placidly cool. Her bearing held a touch of hauteur from generations of landed gentry, that if she only knew, heightened her appeal for the uncouth theater owner.

"Forgive me for disappointing you, Mr. Winestable, but I cannot accept your offer." Jena spoke quietly, her well-bred voice a vivid contrast to her tawdry surroundings. "I have no desire to appear on your stage, either now or at any future date."

"Lord love ya, gel," Winestable snorted. It was almost laughable, he thought in disbelief. The girl's clothes were threadbare, her shoes worn, and her once soft hands rough from her work, and yet she bristled like a princess as she refused his offer. It was like that with all the nobs. Thought they was too bleedin' good for the likes of him. His jowled face took on a crafty look as he glared at the girl. "I'll be leavin' the offer open, out of the kindness of me 'eart. But don't wait too long afore you come arunnin'."

Swiveling around on his heel, he strode angrily to the door. He stood in the doorway hesitantly, then turned back as though he had forgotten something.

"Did I tell you that I won't be needin' you after this week?" he asked, his expression sorrowful but his eyes relishing the shocked look on the women's faces.

"But, Mr. Winestable," Jena cried, leaping to her feet, "you told us last week that you were pleased with our work."

"That be last week, Missy," Winestable chuckled. "Me cousin's daughter is just up from the country and she sews a treat. And as she'll be needin' a job . . ." Winestable's voice trailed off in a low mumble as he left the room.

Jena stood as though transfixed, the pink dress she had been sewing clutched tightly to her bosom and her eyes still staring at the empty doorway. Then on a slow moan, she dropped slowly back onto the stool. Her hands shook and she clenched them tightly in the pile of pink netting. Anger washed over her and she wanted nothing more than to rip the inoffensive dress to pieces. But poverty left little room for anger, either.

"Oh, Nanny, whatever are we going to do?" Jena asked, turning to the older woman.

Resting her mobcapped head against the back of the chair, Nanny gently rocked to and fro. Her eyes were closed and she hummed softly under her breath. Her wrinkled face was pale, with two spots of color high on her cheekbones. Lulled by the rhythm of the chair and the soft lullaby, the tight knot of pain within Jena's breast began to ease. She unclenched her hands and shook out the dress, folding it carefully before she put it down beside the sewing basket. When she looked again, Nanny's eyes were open.

"The man's a bounder," Nanny said. "Mischief weights his footsteps."

Remembering the weight of Mr. Winestable, Jena snorted at the aptness of Nanny's words. She suspected that wasn't exactly what the old woman meant, but the amusing thought did much to bring Jena's own thoughts back to a more reasonable level.

"What if I took the part in the play?" Jena said thoughtfully, avoiding the older woman's eyes as she spoke. "He's only letting us go to force me into it. If I agreed to do the play, I'd insist that he keep you on as seamstress. I don't really do much of the sewing to earn my pay. And just think of it, Nanny, we'd have lots of money. We could buy some new clothes and some boots. We might even be able to find better lodgings."

Jena lifted her head and her voice trailed away at the narrow-eyed gaze of the older woman. She felt as though she were back in the nursery when Nanny had caught her telling a lie. Now as then, the woman had never leavened her words.

"Jena Christie! Never did I think I'd live to see the day when you would give up your principles for an extra crust of bread. Better to die with honor than live with shame, is what I say." Nanny's voice softened as she looked into the stricken girl's eyes. "Sweetheart, never think that you can touch evil and not be tainted. You've lived your life with high principles, and death would be more kind to you than your own conscience. If you became an actress, you'd die a little bit each day."

"I know, Nanny," Jena admitted. "Don't listen to me. Tonight I'm just feeling depressed. Everything will look better tomorrow. We'll just have to look for another job."

But in her heart, Jena acknowledged that their chances of finding another position were very slim. They had searched desperately for honorable employment and had only taken the job in the theater out of desperation. Despite Nanny's harsh words, Jena wondered if death was really preferable to compromising one's ideals. If she were on her own, perhaps she could genteelly fold her hands and waste away, but she had Nanny to consider. The older woman could have found employment, at least enough to keep herself in food and lodgings. But since they had come to London, it was Nanny's sewing talents that had found them work. At sixty, the burden was too much. Ever since Jena was a baby, and Nanny in charge of the nursery, the old woman had loved and cared for the motherless child. Now it was Jena's turn. Somehow she had to find a way to take care of Nanny.

Chapter Two

Lord Devereaux Havenhurst, Viscount Badderley, wearily leaned his head against the high, carved back of his chair. His steely blue eyes flickered around the private parlor and coldly surveyed the oak table littered with bottles, decanters, and the remains of a hearty dinner. Light from the fireplace refracted off the crystal glasses, some half-empty and forgotten, others shining and waiting to be filled. Uncoiling his long legs, Dev straightened his six-foot frame, feeling stiff from an evening of inactivity. He had spent a month hunting at his grandfather's estate, and already regretted exchanging the outdoor freedom for the confinement of society in London.

Damn the interfering old man, Dev muttered under his breath. His face darkened with a blaze of anger before he quickly controlled his emotions, his expression once more hard and cynical. Dev raised the crystal snifter of brandy to his nose, letting the fumes fill his head before he touched the liquor to his tongue. Inhaling deeply, he closed his eyes and savored the sharp bite of the alcohol. Slowly his eyelids lifted and he turned to his three companions. As he focused on each of his friends, a twinkle of approval appeared in Dev's gaze and his expression lightened.

On his left sat Lord Maxwell Kampford, Dev's friend since childhood. It was hard to see in Max's dandified appearance the scruffy boy who had shared many an adventure. His foppish mannerisms caused some to underrate the intelligence behind Max's lazily lowered eyelids.

"Gentlemen, your attention please," Max said, tapping his knife against a nearby wine bottle. With the careful precision of one well under the hatches, he enunciated each word. "The Gray Fox has rejoined us."

One sardonically raised black eyebrow acknowledged the nickname. At the tender age of twenty, Dev's thick black hair had turned gray at the temples. Now at thirty, his shaggy hair was a startling white in striking contrast to his black brows and eyelashes.

"I say, we ought to drink a toast to Dev's return," Lord Reginald Flynn said, nudging the arm of the enormous man hunched over the end of the table. Reggie, his cherubic blond curls falling in wild disarray around his ears, peered owlishly at his cousin, Lord Richard Rice. "Come on, Dickon. You can't fall asleep yet."

"Not asleep, you clapjaw," Dickon growled, yawning hugely. "Sides, we've drunk to Dev's return. Twice. Once to Prinny. Once to Max's new bootmaker and once to my horse. Not much we haven't drunk to."

Reggie nodded his head sagely, running his fingers through his rumpled curls for inspiration. Suddenly he leaped up, knocking over his chair and flailing his arms wildly to maintain his balance. Once steady, he waited while Dickon and Max stumbled to their feet.

"A toast to the Duke of Wayfield!" Reggie shouted.

"Here. Here," Dickon and Max mumbled, but there was no movement to indicate the viscount had even heard the salutation.

"Surely, Dev, you would drink to your grandfather!" Dickon's booming words were slurred as he glowered down at the seated figure.

"For your information, gentlemen, my grandfather and I are no longer on speaking terms." Dev's expression turned flinty as he remembered the sharp exchange of words preceding his return to London. He waited while the grumbling men returned to their seats before coughing politely to regain their attention. Then Dev placed his elbows on the table, leaning toward his friends, who obligingly bent forward, heads together to accept his confidence. Even in their advanced state of insobriety they were eager to understand what circumstances had brought their boyhood chum to such a pass. "My grandfather tried to force me to marry."

"Devil, you say!" Max nervously flicked an invisible speck of lint off his Pomona green satin sleeve.

With sausagelike fingers, Dickon opened the buttons on his already straining waistcoat and pushed the material aside to give his immense girth ample room. "Lud, Dev, the old boy's going too far! Marry, indeed!" Then his enormous arm swept forward, curling possessively around his trencher as though some unknown female were already caviling at the size of his appetite.

Reggie looked appalled at the notion of a woman intruding on their carefree horizons. Although Dev and Max were thirty, he and Dickon were only twenty-seven, much too young to contemplate setting up their nurseries. He shook his blond head at the sudden realization that eventually one of their stalwart number would fall to parson's mousetrap.

Silence filled the room as each of the members of the party examined the bleak, yet inevitable future. The surety of petticoat rule dawned as an abyss before their horrified vision.

Dev tilted his head and cupped his chin in the palm of one hand, staring thoughtfully around the table. "My grandfather has badgered me for years to marry, convinced that the love of a good woman will reform me. During my visit to Wayfield, there was the usual round of parties. A neighbor—a middle-aged harpy if I've ever seen one—discovered me embracing her daughter." At the whoops of gusty laughter, the viscount raised a restraining hand. "A kiss, gentlemen. Nothing more."

"Good Lord, Dev!" Reggie muttered in dismay. Then his brown eyes twinkled knowingly and he leaned confidentially toward his friend. "Was it Lucy Wilsop? That chit's heels are so round she falls over when a coach passes."

Dickon waved a large chunk of bread in Dev's general direction, but as Max reached out a hand, the large man glowered and snatched the crust back, cradling it lovingly against his chest. "Is that the wench who joined us in that epic bacchanalian romp two years ago? Practically wore Reggie to a shadow."

"She never did!" Reggie shouted, his boyish face taking on an injured look as he pointed an accusatory finger at Dickon. "It was you, you great lummox, who climbed to the roof with the girl—"

"Gentlemen. Gentlemen," Dev interjected hastily, realizing that after an evening of drinking, tempers became exceedingly short. "Let us return to my story. It was not Lucy, more's the pity. Even Grandfather wouldn't have been on his high ropes over that girl. It was a young lady of quite unimpeachable pedigree. An ornament of the *ton* and a jewel of great worth to her family. The girl's mother demanded I marry her daughter before word leaked out and irreparable damage was done to her reputation. The girl, alas, did nothing but cry and lament the loss of her innocence. Though Lord knows why, since all I did was kiss her."

"I say, Dev, untried maidens have never been much in your line," Max said. He fastidiously wiped the table in front of him with a lace-edged handkerchief and then leaned forward on one satin-clad elbow as he stared down the table at his friend. "Whole thing sounds positively havey-cavey."

"You have the right of it," Dev said, his voice harsh as his face darkened with remembered anger. "Felt much like a setup. With my wealth and title the ultimate prize."

Dev drew himself up, his long fingers clenched on the carved arms of the chair. The strongly muscled body that made Weston hungry for his custom was poised on the edge of violence. His blue eyes held a shadow of bitterness, clouding the intelligence and humor that generally resided within his honest gaze.

"Nothing's sacred," Reggie mumbled, his voice filled with righteous indignation. He raked impatiently at his blond curls, which a short time ago had been so artfully arranged. "Surely you explained the situation to your grandfather?"

"I informed the duke of exactly what had occurred and voiced my suspicions. However, Grandfather thought he'd discovered the perfect lever to force my marriage. He proclaimed, quite loudly in fact, that I must marry the girl or never darken his door again." Dev's eyes glowed with anger although his voice was soft in the tense room.

"And?" three voices rang out, breaking the expectant silence.

Dev calmly brushed the hair away from his forehead. His fingers were inordinately long and supple, with no tufts of hair to break the clean lines. Their very smoothness hinted at a sensuality and gentleness that was almost visible, yet for all that, there was a deceptive strength beneath the surface. With an abrupt gesture, both hands slapped down on the edge of the table. "I informed the duke that I would have none of it! I will not marry!"

This pronouncement brought cheers and huzzahs from the assemblage and quite naturally a celebratory round of drinks. Dev smiled thinly at the congratulations for his determination and adherence to principles. It was several minutes before he was able to continue.

"I explained to my grandfather that nothing transpired to demand that I do the honorable thing, but he preferred to see it otherwise. When I informed him that I had no intention of marrying the chit, he was furious. He said he wanted me to marry immediately. In fact, his very words were, 'I demand that you marry. I don't care if the girl's an actress, just marry!' "

"An actress?" Dickon snorted. "That's coming it a bit strong."

"A lady or an actress? There's very little difference," Dev said. "They both are interested only in financial gain."

"I agree!" Max applauded delicately, careful not to crumple the lace at his wrists. "My little opera dancer has been hinting that rubies would be perfect against her skin. Or diamonds, or emeralds. After all, gentlemen, one must pay for one's pleasure."

"But not in marriage," Dev said. "Just look at

17

all our friends who have married. Lord knows they've been paying, yet I see damn little pleasure. They all turn into the veriest dullards, living each day in the most frightful respectability, devoid of humor, happiness, or enjoyment."

"What about Louis Revenal?" Reggie asked, mentioning a mutual friend.

"Don't count." Dickon brushed an accumulation of crumbs off his cravat before he continued. "Man's a Frenchie. Foreigners always seem to be having fun."

"Point well taken, cuz," Reggie replied. "I venture to say, though, that if you were in love with the girl, it might make a difference."

"Love!" Dev's voice was harsh as he bit off the word. "I've seen what can happen if you love a woman, and I'll be damned if I ever put myself at such risk."

Dev pushed himself away from the table, walking across the room to stare out of the darkened window. He saw none of the passing activity; his eyes were focused inward remembering his parents' marriage.

His father, Charles Douglas Havenhurst, had fallen in love with his wife-to-be at her come-out ball. The willowy, golden-haired Camilla had had the face of an ethereal goddess. However, more earthly pleasures ruled her life. Raised by a parsimonious father, she was starved for possessions. She had delighted in the clothes and jewels that Charles could provide, and used her body to cajole him to excessive spending. She adored the London social scene and was appalled when she discovered she was expecting a child. A diamond and ruby necklace and a matched set of high-stepping grays consoled her during her dull sojourn in the country until Dev's birth. In this instance Charles felt the expenditure was well justified.

As a boy, Dev had seen little of his mother, who had neither inclination nor patience for nurturing. He spent most of his time trotting after his father. Charles had been a bluff, handsome man, more at home in the saddle than in the drawing room. Aside from his son and his hunting dogs, Camilla was his ruling passion. With a child's judgmental vision he had watched his much-loved father turn into a harried, jealous man, totally under the control of his acquisitive mother. When Charles refused her a bauble, the goddess Camilla flirted with other gentlemen until, magically, the jewel appeared. For a time she would be content until another extravagance caught her eye. Her greed nearly bankrupted the estate. Only his parents' death in a carriage accident had preserved Dev's inheritance.

At nineteen Dev became heir to a title and a considerable fortune. Welcomed into the world of society, he had been besieged by avaricious women, anxious to form an attachment. A rainbow of petticoats fluttered around him, running the gamut from hard-faced, ambitious mothers and their simpering, mindless daughters, to the more exotic enticements of a bevy of flinty-eyed Cyprians. Actress or lady, they all strove to control him and, of prime importance, his money, through empty promises of love. But Dev had sworn he would never fall in love. He would control his own life, taking pleasure wherever he found it.

"When does the duke arrive?"

Max's question dragged Dev back to the present, and he returned to the table. "You know my grandfather. He's all thunder and fire," Dev said, reseating himself. "If he follows his usual pattern, he will have spent most of today harassing the servants.

Henri, the duke's estimable chef, will threaten to quit, and at least three of the housemaids will be in tears. Tonight Trevors, his toplofty butler, will oversee the dinner personally and keep grandfather's glass well filled. Then tomorrow he will wake up with a raging hangover and remember all of my past sins. At that point he will shout out the carriage and arrive on my doorstep as early as possible to deliver a blistering lecture on how I have dishonored the family name."

The men laughed, having been on the wrong end of several of the duke's tirades. Despite the old man's gruff manner, they liked and respected him. But, by and large, the three friends were relieved they would not be facing the fire-breathing duke the next day. Broaching another bottle, they drank companionably as they exchanged words of encouragement with Dev.

"The duke will be more determined than ever to see you married," Reggie said, casting a worried glance at his friend.

"Never fear," Dev said. "I shall inform him once again that I never intend to marry."

"I applaud your firm stand, old man," Max drawled. "Although I hate to bring up such an unwelcome thought, have you considered the dreadful consequences in the untimely, not to mention much regretted, event of your death? With you gone, the direct line will die out. And you know what that means." Max waved his handkerchief before his nose as though smelling a foul odor.

"Ponsonby!" Four voices exhaled the name, their tone clearly indicating the disgust they felt for the owner.

"Your cousin will then become the duke's heir." Dickon spoke aloud the others' thoughts.

"That cit!" Reggie grumbled. "It's been bad

enough that we have to recognize him for the sake of your blue eyes, Dev. But this is coming it too raw. Can you imagine that pompous ass as the next Duke of Wayfield?"

Depression settled over the private room as each of the men contemplated life with Edward Ponsonby as a member of the nobility.

"By Gad, sirs, I have just the answer!" Reggie shouted, smiling broadly at his friends' startled expressions.

With proper dignity, Reggie wove to his feet, bracing himself with one hand on a nearby decanter of brandy. He cocked his head in surprise as though seeing the alcohol for the first time and, catching up the bottle, lifted it to his lips for a restorative sample. Thus fortified, he continued, "Dev must marry and beget an heir."

The sheer idiocy of the suggestion brought immediate catcalls. Suddenly a sharp crack of laughter burst from Dev and the anger that had plagued him all evening seemed to slip away. "You have hit on the perfect plan to get back at my interfering grandfather," Dev said.

"Get back at the man?" Max asked in amazement. "He *wants* you to marry!"

"Exactly!" There was a definite slyness to the grin on the Gray Fox's face. "And I plan to give my grandfather his fondest wish."

"Devil take it, old man," Dickon muttered, his eyebrows bunched in concern. "It does seem an extreme solution. Wouldn't lesser measures do as well?"

"No, my friends. It's just the ticket. I must secure the line," Dev intoned solemnly. "Will you drink with me?"

"Well done, Dev," Reggie said, gripping his friend's shoulder happily, although there did seem

21

to be a moist look to his brown eyes as he contemplated how much Dev was willing to sacrifice to save them from the embarrassment of Ponsonby.

"You've always been willing to do the right thing," Max said, gripping Dev's hand in an excess of emotion. "First standing up to your grandfather, and now marriage."

The three men stared down at Dickon, whose eyes were still glued to his half-empty trencher. The large man groggily raised his head, his eyes unreadable as he studied his friends. Then in a majestic gesture, he pushed his plate into the center of the table and rose to his feet. Solemnly he wiped his mouth, throwing the napkin onto the littered table.

"We've stood together before, Dev," Dickon proclaimed. "I'll not fail you now."

The four men steadied themselves on each others' shoulders as they raised fresh glasses and solemnly drank. One after the other they flung their snifters into the fire, sending the flames shooting upward in a burst of alcoholic spray. In the silence that followed they sank into their chairs, feeling ennobled by their gesture. Since most of their adventures had been in each other's company, it did not occur to any of the four that Dev should take on this heavy burden of responsibility alone. Putting their heads together, they would outline a plan of attack that would dazzle the most hardened military tacticians.

"Our first objective must be Almack's," Reggie said, tugging pensively at his earlobe.

"Do you think Sally Jersey has forgiven us for the last time we entered those august portals?" Dickon added.

"I don't see why Dev and I should be tarred with that brush of scandal," Max said, leaning forward

22

to glare at Dickon. "It was your idea to add the spirits to the lemonade. I was having my jacket creased by the grip of that Amazon from Bath."

"I remember," Reggie said, his teeth flashing in a wide grin. "Patience Atwater. Had the arms of a pot scrubber and the face of a pugilist. They were making their come-out. She and her sister Chastity."

"A poorly named baggage, if there ever was one," Dickon intoned, plump finger tapping the side of his nose.

"Never say, you old libertine!" Max crowed.

"I am sorely injured that you did not confide in me, cuz," Reggie said.

"Thought I had," Dickon said, shaking his head as though to dredge up the memory. "It was at Hewitt-Armstrong's. The naughty minx dragged me into the bushes."

"Gentlemen! Gentlemen!" Dev interrupted. "I would dearly love to be privy to Dickon's unbridled gropings, but we must get back to the problem at hand."

"Sorry, old man," Max said, glaring around the table as if to stiffen their resolve.

"We must implement our plan this very evening," Dev announced decisively.

"Good Lord, Dev," Reggie said, his voice hesitant as he viewed the magnitude of this undertaking. "Surely there's no need to be quite so precipitate."

"My grandfather will be arriving tomorrow. I would like to present him with a *fait accompli*." Dev grinned around the table. "After all, gentlemen, once I marry and beget an heir, I will have done my duty and will be free to continue my life."

"Good point, old man," Max agreed.

"Now, as I see it, gentlemen, our first problem is

23

who will do the marrying on such short notice? And second, where can we obtain a special license?"

Max raised a languid hand to catch Dev's attention. "I think I can be of some small assistance in the little matter of the license." Slipping an elegant hand inside his multicolored brocade waistcoat, he slowly extracted a folded paper. With exaggerated care he spread the parchment on the table, smoothing his hand across the scrolled writing. He smiled broadly at the sigh of satisfaction from the others.

"What are you doing with a special license?" Dickon accused, glowering across at his dapper friend.

"My brother was threatening to marry that shop assistant he's been mooning after unless I permitted him to purchase Whitticker's bays. He got the cattle and I got the license." Max sighed philosophically at the antics of twenty year olds.

"Good show, Max," Reggie exclaimed. "And speaking of brothers, we'll rout out mine for the ceremony. I knew having a vicar in the family would come in handy one day."

"Now all we need is the blushing bride," Dickon said.

"Where are we going to come up with a delightful, respectable deb on such short notice?" Reggie asked, looking in consternation around the table.

"Why, surely you remember the duke's suggestion," Dev said, his blue eyes alight with mischief, drawing answering grins from the others. "After all, if he doesn't care if I marry an actress, then, like an obedient grandson, I will marry on actress."

"An actress! By Jove, you've got it," Reggie said, his voice awed at the perspicacity of his friend.

"Seems a bit extreme, even to spite the duke. But, as always, I am yours to command." Max shrugged and pulled out his timepiece, squinting his eyes to read the wavering numbers. "The theaters will be closing in another hour, old boy. Not much time to pick out a bride."

"No time to pick one, Max." Dev said. "We'll just have to settle for the first one we see. Remember, I have to marry her, but I don't have to live with her. I'll hide her away on one of my estates up north. With the Devil's luck, I might never have to see her again until she's old and gray. Then it won't matter."

"Good point, Dev," Reggie applauded. "Well, we better be off. The bride awaits. And time is short."

"Quite correct. After all, gentlemen, I have not only to marry, but beget an heir," Dev said, his mouth curving into a smile of triumph. "Tonight I will do my duty by the line. Thus, tomorrow I will be free to get on with my life."

Chapter Three

"That's the last of the sewing, Nanny," Jena said as she hung the gypsy shawl on the costume rod.

Her eyes flickered along the row of tawdry dresses, delighting in the kaleidoscope of gaudy colors. Up close, most of the gowns were makeshift, poorly sewn and cheaply made, the fabrics inferior quality. But beneath the stage lights, the gowns magically took on an elegance, due mainly to the pure jewel tones of the colors. Against the lush display, Jena's dun-colored dress looked even more threadbare than usual. Sighing tiredly, she stretched her arms over her head, rolling her shoulders to ease the stiffness in her back.

"Don't dawdle, Miss Jena. Come and git your cape," Nanny muttered as she replaced the needles and thread in the sewing basket. She shook her skirts, brushing at the tufts of fabric that clung to the front of her smock.

Jena reached for her dark wool cape and flung it around her shoulders. Crossing the room, she wrapped Nanny gently in the serviceable knitted shawl that the old woman preferred. Then she opened the door and paused for a moment to catch the naughty refrain being sung onstage. She cocked her head, chuckling at the risqué lyrics. At the shocked look on her companion's face, Jena laughed aloud, then turned as the affronted woman prodded her toward the back door of the theater.

"We're late tonight. We should have left twenty minutes ago," Nanny snapped. "I don't like you out on the streets when the theaters empty. Wine and wealth change wise men's manners, is what I say."

"Don't worry. I'm coming." Jena ignored Nanny's cross tones, knowing the gruffness was a combination of worry and exhaustion. "I'll fix us a nice cup of tea when we get home."

"Hurry now, child, and be sure you pull the hood well over your hair."

Nanny had warned Jena continuously about the dangerous and immoral conduct of the denizens of the night. For the most part the women had been lucky. Their unfashionable clothes and obvious lack of wealth had convinced the sneak thieves they possessed little of value. The most persistent hazard of working in the theater district was the prevalence of roistering gentlemen who prowled the area on the lookout for women of easy, though seldom inexpensive, virtue. Several times, Jena and Nanny had run the gauntlet of society rakes bent on an evening of pleasure. Generally they had little trouble evading them.

Jena tucked her thick braid of black hair beneath her hood and followed Nanny's plump little figure. Stepping out the back door of the theater, the women paused on the top step and sniffed, gratefully inhaling the night air. Jena ignored the sharp bite of the March wind that blew against her hot cheeks.

"You can almost smell spring in the air, Nanny."

"All I smell is dead cats and yesterday's garbage," the old woman muttered, huddling deeper within her shawl.

27

Undaunted, Jena raised her face to the night sky and inhaled again, filling her lungs and reveling in the breeze on her skin. Spring was her favorite time of year. It was a time of hope and new life. The mares would be dropping foals, each one a miraculous combination of its dam and sire. If only . . . Jena hunched her shoulders, suddenly aware of the cutting chill to the wind. There was no time for "if onlys" in her new life. Slowly her eyes dropped from the clear night sky and returned to the noisome alleyway.

Far down the narrow walkway, light beckoned where the alley joined the street. The women kept to the center of the cobblestones, cautiously picking their way past unknown bundles thrown haphazardly against the walls of the surrounding buildings. The scrabble of invisible feet made Jena shudder and she tried not to picture what loathsome vermin had crossed her path. They were almost at the end of the alley when a solid wall of figures abruptly blotted out the light.

"Tallyho, ladies," one of the figures shouted, his voice echoing hollowly against the grimy buildings.

Nanny immediately pushed Jena behind her and confronted the men. "Git on along, you loiterers. Don't you be blocking honest women from going home after work." She turned around and pulled Jena's hood more closely around her face. "Come along, dearie. We'll soon be home and get a nice hot cuppa."

Jena was not as frightened as she had been the first time that they had been accosted by young gallants waiting for the actresses to come out of the theater. Pretending they were old women, exhausted by their labors, had been enough to discourage the men. Now, like a seasoned actress, Jena kept her head bent and shuffled her feet like the

28

old women she had seen. Under the protection of her hood, she eyed the gentlemen who had stepped aside to let them pass.

A caped dandy in a bilious green suit waved a perfumed handkerchief in front of his nose as though the two women smelled as rank as the alleyway. "On your way, goodwives. We're looking for more tender morsels than you two."

A veritable giant, his round face split in a fatuous grin, squinted owlishly at Jena and she huddled within her cape, aware of the thinness of her disguise. The third man, a curly-headed blonde, made an elegant leg, although this flawlessly executed obeisance was slightly marred when he had difficulty maintaining his balance.

"Good evening, ladies," the blonde said. "Or perhaps I should wish you good morning."

"I wish you to perdition," Nanny muttered under her breath as she clutched Jena's arm and hustled her toward the safety of the street.

Jena was too close now to risk looking up at the fourth man. Her heart thundered in her ears as she hurried past him. In her enthusiasm for the play-acting, her foot caught on a rough stone and she tripped. Jena flung her hands out to break the fall, grateful for the protection of her mittens as she stumbled to her hands and knees. The fall took her breath away and she stretched her head back to fill her lungs with air. It was Nanny's gasp of fear that alerted Jena to her danger. Her hand groped for the security of her hood, but it was too late. Her braid of black hair and youthful face were exposed to the astonished eyes of the men, who instantly surrounded her fallen figure.

"I say, Dev," a deep voice drawled as the men circled closer. "I do believe we've found ourselves a bird."

"Don't you touch my lady," Nanny screeched, pushing her way between the ring of men and standing like an avenging angel beside Jena. "Go on with you or I'll scream for the watch."

Ignoring the old woman's scolding voice, the men extended their hands and Jena was raised to her feet. She felt suffocated by the closeness of the men and fought to catch her breath. Her heart jolted in fear as they pressed around her, but, as though she were a child, they solicitously brushed her cape free of the dirt and grime from the cobblestones.

"Are you hurt, miss?" the giant asked. He grasped Jena's hands and peeled off the soiled mittens, flinging them to the ground in disgust. Carefully he examined the palms of her hands, then reached out as though he might personally inspect the rest of her body.

"Please!" Jena staggered back, slapping at the enormous groping hands. "Thank you, but I'm fine."

"Good show," the cheerful blonde said. "We wouldn't want damaged goods." At his own words he guffawed loudly.

Hearing Nanny's moan of fear, Jena pulled her scattered wits together. This was no place for either of them. It was obvious by their behavior that the men were foxed, but at least they did not appear to be particularly menacing. "We want no trouble, sirs. Please let us pass."

Grinning broadly, the green popinjay bowed deeply in her direction. "Your pardon, ladies. We would be proud to escort you to a hackney."

"That won't be necessary," Jena said, her voice cold as she tried to withdraw from the men. She pushed her way to Nanny, putting her arm around the old woman's shoulder. At the trembling of her friend, she glared at the men, furious that they

30

would frighten the woman. "We do not desire a carriage. Please leave us alone."

Jena turned toward the street, but the fourth man blocked her path. Throughout the confrontation with the other men, Jena had been aware of his presence. He had taken no part in the conversation, but his very silence had drawn her attention. He had an air of control that contrasted sharply with the more befuddled behavior of his comrades.

Slowly Jena's eyes scanned his figure. He was tall and, beneath a dark greatcoat, fashionably dressed in dark blue satin. When she noticed his white hair, she assumed he was older and opened her mouth to appeal for help. But on closer inspection she registered the smooth, tanned skin and the sharply defined features of his face. She started to speak, but her breath caught in her throat as her eyes locked with the man's piercing blue gaze. For a moment she had the sensation of falling, and her stomach lurched in response. Her heartbeat quickened and she found it impossible to look away. There was some quality in the white-haired man's face that reached out to her, and despite the hawkish features, she was not afraid.

Lord Devereaux Havenhurst sighed in pure pleasure as he stared down into the huge gray eyes of the girl. Although only seconds had elapsed, Dev knew that he would be able to describe her every feature, so clearly were they imprinted on his mind. Petal-soft skin, high cheekbones, ebony hair, and enormous eyes under gracefully arched brows. He had seen more beautiful women, but there was an aura that surrounded the actress that sent his senses reeling. As he continued to feast his eyes on the girl, the alcoholic fumes swirling in his head dissipated and he quickly made a decision.

On Dev's signal, the other men closed in around

31

the two women. Like well-trained sheepdogs, Max and Reggie separated the old lady from the actress. Dev reached for the arm of the young girl as Dickon attached himself to her other side. Their booted steps were muffled by the redolent garbage as they marched down the alley in close formation.

Wedged tightly between the white-haired man and the giant, Jena found herself panting but was unable to slow because of the helpful hands cupping her elbows. A frantic glance over her shoulder reassured her that Nanny was following with the other two gentlemen. For all their show of fine manners, there was danger inherent in the situation. With relief, she spotted the hackney pulled up at the curb. This was no time to worry about the expense of a cab. The quicker she and Nanny could get away from the men, the happier Jena would be. As they emerged into the night-darkened street, the giant bounded forward to swing open the door of the hackney. Jena placed her foot on the first step and turned to the white-haired man.

"Thank you—" Jena's words were cut off as the men surged forward, trying to force their way into the carriage with her. Panic threatened to engulf her as they pressed around her. She kicked out, straining away from the open door and slapping at the hands trying to imprison her. As Jena fought, Nanny became aware of what was happening and began to set up a row.

"Help! Help! Send for the guard!" Nanny screamed, pounding on the back of the short, elegantly dressed man.

"Stubble her, Max!" Dev shouted as he tried to pull Jena into the cab. Over his shoulder, he watched in amazement as the feisty old lady danced between Max and Reggie. All the time her arms flailed, she screeched for help. Dev freed one hand from the struggling girl and pushed Dickon in the direction of the caterwauling Nanny. "I'll take care of this one, Dickon. You give them a hand."

As the large man lumbered forward, the little old lady raised her fist and punched him in the nose. He reeled away howling and she continued to struggle with the fastidious Max. When she tore away his cravat, he, too, backed away, staring in stupefaction at her hand where she waved the crumpled piece of linen.

"Let go of me!" Jena cried as she fought desperately to escape. Although her captor was six feet tall, she reached up, trying to scratch his face. One hand connected and she felt a surge of satisfaction when the man yelped as her nails scraped along his cheek. He staggered backward and Jena managed to pull herself free. Suddenly the blond nobleman appeared at her side. He grabbed one of her hands, but she leaned forward, planting her teeth in his wrist. He snatched his hand away, waving his throbbing arm and examining the bite marks with horror.

Once more Jena attempted to escape, but muscular arms crushed her to a hard chest, and she looked up into the face of the white-haired man. Although hampered by her skirts, she was able to raise her foot and kick him in the ankle. Grunting in pain, Dev released her immediately, hopping awkwardly on the other foot. He bent forward and Jena grabbed a handful of hair and tried to bang his head against the side of the coach.

"Driver," she shrieked. "Please help us."

The hackney driver stared down at the scene of mayhem with a totally bemused expression on his face. The reins lay slack across his lap and he leaned casually against the whip stand. Even in the flickering moonlight, Jena could see the absolute lack of tension in the figure, as though set apart and watching some sort of street performance.

"You're doing just fine, missy." The driver hawked and spit over the backs of the docile livery horses.

Dev shook his head, trying to dislodge the girl's hands. With a roar of pain as the contrary wench yanked once more on his hair, he gripped her wrists, pulling the offending weapons away from his much-abused scalp. Concentrating, he managed to capture her flailing arms, and pinned them to her sides. He released them quickly, pulling the folds of her cape around her body, effectively imprisoning the wriggling girl inside the material. He slumped against the side of the hackney, staring over the actress's head at the melee in progress.

Reggie had reentered the fray with the old woman. "Come on, mother. Don't take on so." Warily, he circled around the savage little woman. "Give over."

While Dev watched in frustration, Reggie attempted to grab hold of the old woman's arm, but she kept dodging around, punching at his extended arm. Max mournfully beheld his decapitated cravat, which lay terminally limp across his opened palms. Even Dickon had been routed. He weaved back and forth on the walk, dabbing gingerly at his bleeding nose, a sound much like the mewling of an injured kitten issuing from his throat.

"A Wayfield!" Dev cried.

At the ancient battle cry, his three confederates snapped to attention, staring blearily at their commander. The old woman began to scream once more.

"Murder! Save us!"

"Devil take it, men. Get that woman and bring

34

her along." As they hesitated, Dev rapped out in a voice reminiscent of England's finest, "Charge!"

Max and Reggie pounced on the old woman, grabbing for her thrashing arms. Dickon delayed long enough to undo his cloak and drop it over the shouting woman's head. The screams effectively muffled, he wrapped his enormous arms around the little figure and hoisted her to his shoulder. Max and Reggie, a much battered guard of honor, led the way to the carriage. Dev picked up the girl and stepped up into the hackney as the others, bearing their writhing burden, followed suit. As the door swung shut, the driver gave the horses the office to start. The carriage leaped forward and Reggie and Max were flung on top of Dev and the girl.

"Get off me, you gudgeon." Dev's voice came muffled from the pileup. "Don't hurt the girl."

"Ow! Watch your elbow, Reggie. What a great looby you are!" Max pushed himself upright, hitting his head a smart crack on the ceiling of the coach. Moaning, he collapsed on the seat beside a grinning Dickon and the snarling bundle he had clamped tightly to his side. The fashionable young man recoiled from the old woman, pressing his body into the corner of the coach.

"Good show, Dev," Reggie chuckled as he settled in the seat beside his friend and the wide-eyed girl. "Haven't had this kind of action since our school days. Such teamwork."

"Stow it, you idiot. We almost muffed the whole affair," Dev snapped. "Just look at the lot of us. What dashing adventurers!"

There was silence in the coach as four pairs of eyes surveyed their injuries and the total wreckage of their attire. Dev smiled grimly at the devastation that had been wrought by two fragile-looking women. Dickon's nose had bled down the front of his waistcoat, and his linen could be no more blood-soaked if his throat had been cut. Max was without a cravat, although, loyal to the end, he still clutched the rumpled item in his fist. One of the short capes of his multicaped greatcoat had been torn away entirely, while another dangled in tattered disarray to below his knees. Reggie, at first glance, seemed to have received little damage, but his cloak was missing and the back seam of his jacket had been split from hem to neck. His blond curls stuck out in loutish clumps, his jawline bore a nasty bruise, and there was an angry ring of tooth marks on his wrist.

As the carriage lurched from side to side, Dev shook his head, glancing down at the ruination of his own clothes. The lapel of his jacket had been shredded, and fluttered like fringe against his waistcoat. His cravat had been torn away, and the right sleeve of his greatcoat had been ripped at the shoulder, falling in rumpled folds to his elbow. He winced at the dirt on his dark blue pantaloons, wondering if his valet would ever speak to him again. He grinned, then grimaced as he felt the scratch on his cheek open and begin to bleed once more. He reached for his handkerchief, gingerly dabbing at the cuts.

Looking up, Dev's eyes crossed with Dickon's, and at the unholy grin of pleasure on the enormous man's face, a chuckle of amusement burst from his lips. At first the sounds in the coach were only sniggers, but as the magnitude of their injuries at the hands of the two women became apparent, the men were overcome with the humor of the situation. They howled like madmen until tears of laughter stood in their eyes.

In the midst of this mayhem, Jena could only exchange wide-eyed glances with Nanny, who had managed to unwind the cloak enough to free her head.

Up until this point Jena had been terrified. Now as she looked around at the hysterical men, she came to the conclusion that the bumbling foursome might be harmless. It was obvious that the noblemen were drunk. She was still afraid; her heart's frantic beat continued to send tremors through her body. The kidnapping had to be a prank of some kind, hatched up over many bottles of spirits. If she and Nanny remained calm, they should be able to reason their way out of the horrible situation. Trying to convey reassurance to the older woman, Jena rested against the squabs, conserving her energy and waiting for the paroxysm of laughter to subside.

"Gentlemen, we must get ourselves in hand," Dev announced, trying to pull himself together. He waggled his eyebrows in the direction of the women, and soon, apart from an occasional snort of amusement, the other three men had controlled their laughter and were busily rearranging their clothing. "We will adjourn to my library, where we can finalize our arrangements and refresh ourselves."

"By Gad, sir. I'm starving," Dickon enthused. "I don't suppose your cook could be routed out of bed to prepare a light snack."

"It's well past midnight, you great lummox." Max yawned, covering his mouth with his ragged cravat. Spying the accusing linen, he sent a glowering look at Nanny, who cowered back against the seat.

"What are we going to do with the old lady, Dev?" Reggie asked. "She's definitely *de trop*."

"We could just toss her out," Dickon suggested, then looked crestfallen when the woman cringed away from him. "Sorry, missus, it just slipped out.

I swear to you, I'd never harm a white hair on your head."

"If we let her go, she'll have the Runners on us before we can even start the ceremony." Reggie pursed his mouth in concentration.

"Well, Dev, what are we going to do with her?" Max persisted.

"I have absolutely no idea," Dev said, massaging the back of his neck to ease his stiffness.

"It's not my fault," Dickon said, his voice loudly defensive. "You told me to bring her."

"The only reason I told you to bring her," Dev said through gritted teeth, "was to stop her cater-wauling. Two more minutes and she'd have had the whole bloody watch down on our heads."

"Excuse me, gentlemen, but we would like to go home," Jena said.

The sound of her quietly spoken words jolted the men. All eyes swung to her with the same amazed attention they would have given to a horse that had just spoken. Jena could feel the color rise in her cheeks under the battery of glances. Reminding herself that she must appear authoritative, as she had when her father was in his cups, Jena straightened her shoulders and pulled herself more erect on the seat.

"We would like to go home," she repeated. "You gentlemen have had your fun, but it is late. We have had a long day of work and would like to return to our lodgings."

"I say, Dev," Reggie said, completely ignoring Jena's words and leaning forward to catch his friend's eye. "She speaks better than most of the, eh, muslin trade."

"She's a rare beauty," Max admitted. He closely examined the girl's flushed face and waxed poetic at her obvious charms. "Hair like midnight and skin like dawn."

"I like her eyes," Dickon added.

"Perhaps you'd like to see my teeth," Jena snapped.

There was silence at her sharp comment, and then the four men burst into laughter.

"How droll, Dev," Max said, winking broadly at his friend. "The lady is possessed of a fine sense of humor. Me thinks she will have need of it before the evening is out."

Jena crossed her arms protectively over her breast, glowering around the crowded carriage. Anger forced fear into the background and she wished there was enough room to kick out in her fury. Suddenly the carriage lurched and she was thrown against the white-haired man, the one the others referred to as Dev. It was evident he was the leader of this incompetent group.

She looked up at him, caught once more by the intensity of his gaze. Her mouth was dry and she licked her lips before she was able to speak. "Please, sir. If you would just set us down, you can return to your entertainments. I am sure there are any number of women who would be delighted to be in the company of such fine gentlemen."

Dev's clear blue eyes twinkled down into Jena's wide smoky gray ones. He cocked his head to the side as though he were giving her suggestion some thought. Then his face took on an expression of almost clownish sadness, and slowly he shook his head.

"I'm sorry to disappoint you, milady," Dev said, his deep-toned voice bearing a funereal note. "But we have gone to so much trouble to find you that I think we better hang on to you. I doubt if this merry

39

little band is up to any more strenuous activity tonight."

Jena's heart sank at Dev's words. She had hoped they would be able to convince the men to release them before they arrived at their destination, but could see now that they would have to bide their time and then attempt an escape. Flashing a warning glance at Nanny, Jena subsided against the seat as the coach slowed and then jerked to a stop.

Chapter Four

Dev inched one eyelid open and suspected that he was dying. At least he hoped he was. Every part of his body ached or throbbed in protest to his slightest movement. He closed his eye, wondering how it was possible to actually feel his hair growing. He shifted his body slightly, sucking in his breath from the pain in his temples where the blood pounded. Damn, but he must have been drunk last night to wake up still sitting in a chair.

Both eyes snapped open and an alarm rang along his nerves. Dev groaned at the agony of each movement. There was something about last night that made his body break out into a sweat. He focused his eyes on the window, wincing at the dawn light filtering through the curtains. Squinting and grimacing, he turned his head slowly on his stiff neck, but found nothing out of place in his bedroom. His questing glance halted at the black velvet hangings on the four-poster bed. Some memory immediately triggered a pounding of his heart, and he pressed a shaking hand to his chest. There was a flash of wide gray eyes in a white, unsmiling face, but when he tried to hold the memory, it disappeared in the muddle of his mind.

Elbows on his knees, Dev dropped his aching head

into his hands. What on earth had they been drinking last night? He had always prided himself on his ability to hold his liquor. He remembered being furious over the imbroglio with his grandfather. He vaguely recalled arguing with his friends about. . . . about joining the army? Oh good Lord, Dev groaned. He might be angry at the duke, but to contemplate joining the army was a bit extreme.

He let his head slump against the cushioned back of the wing chair, pulling resuscitating breaths deep into his lungs. He knew there was something that he needed to remember, and yet his mind seemed reluctant to cooperate. Lethargically his eyes roamed the room for some clue. Nothing appeared different in the bachelor environment.

Bachelor! The word rang a clarion note of distress through his body, and with a jolt, memory returned. Last night he, Lord Devereaux Havenhurst, Viscount Badderley, heir to the Duke of Wayfield, had married an actress picked up off the streets of London.

"God's holy breath!" he swore.

Snatches of the bizarre scene in the library returned in agonizing clarity. Reggie's brother, the vicar, irate that he had been dragged from his bed to perform the havey-cavey ceremony. Max, weaving unsteadily at Dev's side, acting the part of groomsman. Dickon, majestically drunk, bowing awkwardly as he presented red roses, stems still dripping water, which he had plucked from a vase on Dev's desk. There was even an old crone, who snuffled noisily into her ragged shawl. Of the bride, Dev had little remembrance, except for a picture of great pools of gray set in a frightened little face.

The shock of his returning memory cleared away the majority of his hangover. For the first time since he had awakened, his mind was unclouded by the aftermath of his bacchanal. He was appalled that he should have been so beyond himself that he would have participated in a bogus ceremony. Beads of perspiration dotted his upper lip as he recalled that Reggie's brother, the vicar, had cautioned him that the marriage was totally legal. He'd surely landed himself in the basket this time. He must immediately contact his man of business to secure an annulment or whatever was required. My God! He had even planned to beget an heir, he recalled in horror.

At least he hadn't bedded the little tart! Or had he? Forcing his mind back to the painful memories of the night before, he pictured the final scene of the farce. He and his bride had been escorted to his rooms by his sozzled friends and the mewling old lady. Once more Dev caught a faint glimpse of the actress, her slender fingers clinging to the fluted bedpost. He remembered pouring a snifter of brandy and stumbling into the wing chair. He had raised the brandy to his lips, swallowed deeply, and replaced the glass precisely in the center of the side table. Then raising his eyes to the young woman beside the bed, he had been surprised when her form wavered, filtering away as he sank into blackness.

"Damnation!" Dev swore at the humiliating memory. He could not believe that he had been so badly foxed. In his younger days, he and his cronies had been involved in episodes that were hardly edifying to recall. But at thirty, to behave in such a rackety fashion was demoralizing to his self-esteem. He straightened his spine, calling upon his ancient lineage and traditions to armor himself against the consequences of his own stupidity. Without doubt this would be a costly affair. It would be difficult to keep this monumental scandal quiet. He could imagine the blistering lecture that he would receive from his grandfather for creating such a nine days' wonder.

Dev pushed himself to his feet. Dizziness turned his knees to liquid, but force of will kept him upright. He cajoled his feet into crossing the room and pulled the bell rope decisively. He waited stoically for his valet, all the while his mind racing with the implications of his latest folly.

If he presented a cordial face to the actress, he suspected that they should be able to work out an arrangement. He had dealt with enough women in his time to know the magic properties of gold. She would show some reluctance at first in order to keep the price high. But in the end, like her sisters in greed, she would profit immeasurably from Dev's stupidity.

"I must have been cork-brained," Jena moaned, reverting to the cant she had learned at her father's side. "How could I have done something so lack-witted?"

She sat on the window seat staring bleakly out of the window as the first streaks of dawn lit the sky. Slumping wearily against the casement, she followed the progress of a footman methodically sweeping the front stairs of the mansion across the cobblestoned street. She raised a hand to brush the tumbled curls away from her forehead. The sunlight reflected off the gold signet ring on her finger, and she sucked in her breath at the incriminating evidence of her folly. She extended her arm, fingers spread until the skin stretched whitely. The ring slipped forward, covering her knuckle, but remained on her finger, a brand to mark her forever.

She was married to Lord Devereaux Havenhurst, the man who had kidnapped her the night before.

She choked back a hysterical laugh, covering her lips with one clenched fist as she stared down at the ring on her finger.

In the reasonable clarity of morning she was appalled that she had actually agreed to the wedding. With shaking fingers she touched the cold metal of the ring and bent her head as a chill crept into her bones. Behind her closed lids, scenes flashed across her mind as she painfully reviewed the bizarre marriage ceremony in the viscount's library.

Jena would remember the angry face of the vicar forever. He had argued vigorously against the wedding, but his furious words had meant little to the band of roisterers, who were determined that the ceremony would take place. Nanny had clung to Jena to the last minute before the fateful words were spoken. Then, as though the final blessing were an epitaph, her wrinkled face took on a sadly resigned expression, lips puckered in disapproval.

Hands pressed tightly against her shuttered eyes, Jena pictured the bridegroom, and she winced at the remembrance. The tall, elegant, white-haired man had stood beside her with an expression of polite boredom etched on his aristocratic features. His strong fingers held her own with an awkward pressure that, despite the intimate contact, was wholly impersonal. The viscount gave his responses tersely, without glancing once in her direction. At the end of the ceremony, he bowed to the departing vicar, then turned and repeated the obeisance to Jena.

A ragged snore broke into Jena's thoughts. Her eyes flew to the huddled figure in the four-poster. Nanny, still fully dressed, lay snuggled beneath the eiderdown. The old woman was obviously exhausted by the evening's adventures, Jena thought grimly. Good Lord, what a travesty! Her eyes

45

drifted from the bed to the door that connected with her new husband's rooms. Her face burned at the remembrance of the humiliating ending to the evening.

After the stark ceremony, she and the groom had been escorted by their drunken guard of honor to his rooms. Incredibly, after downing a final snifter of brandy, the viscount had fallen asleep in his chair. In relief and embarrassment, Jena had escaped to the bedroom next door and the comfort of Nanny's arms.

Lord, what a coil!

Another snore broke the silence of the room, followed by a snort and a gasping sigh. The bed creaked as Nanny fought against the clinging eiderdown. Jena stood up, crossing to the bed and her awakened companion.

"Good morning, Nanny."

"Jena?" the old woman mumbled querulously as she struggled upright. "Did I dream it all, child?"

"No, I'm afraid it really happened." Jena plumped the pillows against the headboard, pushing open the bed curtains. "Just lie back and catch your breath."

Jena smiled at the lopsided mobcap on her companions's head. Reddened fingers struggled to tuck the white curls beneath the cap, but the old woman's eyes were busy surveying the lavishly decorated room.

"It's a far cry from Mistress McGuire's boardinghouse," Nanny said. "Thought pigs would fly before I'd see the inside of a nob's house again."

Jena snorted, then immediately sobered at the narrow-eyed gaze boring into her. She ducked her head, embarrassed under the old woman's scrutiny.

"Why, child?"

"It was the only answer," Jena said, refusing to

misunderstand Nanny's question. "Last night it seemed perfectly right. It is only with the morning that I find my actions quite incomprehensible."

"We could have found another job," Nanny argued. "Just because that loathsome Mr. Winestable was letting us go! There are other theaters. We would have come about."

Sitting down on the side of the bed, Jena covered the older woman's hands, which were nervously pleating the sheet. She winced at the roughness of the skin, remembering how Nanny's hands had always been soft against Jena's bruised or fevered skin. But that was when she was the pampered daughter of the house. Now she was on her own, having barely a feather to fly with. She must be practical and sanguine about her future.

"We might have found another position, Nanny," Jena said, speaking briskly to convey her decisiveness. "But at best it would only have been a temporary measure. The money from the leasing of Dunton House was practically gone."

"Gone, child?" the woman asked, her voice reflecting the horror of her thoughts. "But it were so much. How is that possible?"

"There always was something," Jena said. She stood up, walking across the beige and blue carpet, her head down as though admiring the pattern. "The tenants and the servants. Money for Widow Mackay. A wet nurse for John Larson's baby. Slates for the schoolhouse. None of them were monstrous expenses, but I could not deny my people."

"Jena, you cannot afford to—"

"Where do I draw the line, Nanny?" Jena interrupted, her voice trembling. "All of these people have worked for and depended on my family for years. I cannot abandon them."

"And so you married a drunken rake in order to protect your people?"

"Yes!" Jena hissed. Whirling around, she faced the bed defiantly. She held her head proudly, although her chin trembled slightly with the surge of fear at her own actions. "It was the only solution."

"Softly, child, softly," Nanny whispered, hearing the cry beneath the sharply spoken words. She patted the bed, and the trembling girl returned, once more taking comfort from the work-reddened hands of her old friend.

"Besides, Nanny, the viscount refused to listen to my entreaties that he release us," Jena continued. "When I realized that he was adamant, I accepted it as a gift from the gods."

"Watch your tongue, missy," Nanny said, crossing herself at the imagined blasphemy.

"At any rate, I really did think it was the answer to my prayers. The viscount appeared to be desperate for a wife. If I refused, there would have been a frightful row. The mere fact that those drunken imbeciles had kidnapped me would have put paid to any scrap of reputation I possessed. Really, Nanny, I had little choice in the matter."

"No need to wrap it up in clean linen, my girl," came the acerbic answer.

"I'm not excusing myself," Jena replied. "Most marriages are arranged on strictly practical lines. I see no reason that this union cannot be viewed as a business arrangement. The wedding itself was legal despite certain irregular aspects of the conditions."

"Kidnapping. Drunkenness. Mere bagatelles!" Nanny moaned. "Thank the good Lord and all His saints that your mother and father cannot witness this day!"

"Nonsense, Nanny," Jena snapped. "Despite the irregularities of the start of this marriage, I fully intend to keep my part of the bargain. I will be a good and faithful wife to the viscount."

"That's all well and good, missy, but what of the bridegroom?" Nanny said. "Have you considered how he intends to conduct himself? If last night is an example of his behavior, I think you will bitterly regret this decision."

"What's done is done, Nanny," Jena said, bowing her head tiredly.

A light scratching at the door brought Jena's head up with a jolt. The muscles tightened in her jawline and she straightened her shoulders as she got up from the bed. Feet dragging in reluctance, she crossed to the door. Opening it, she found a young housemaid.

"Morning, m-madam," the nervous girl stammered, bobbing a slight curtsy. "His lordship asked if you would join him in the morning room to break your fast."

Startled by the request and unsure if she could bear to face the viscount just yet, Jena hesitated. The little housemaid stood blinking in the doorway like an inquisitive owl. Knowing there was nothing to be gained by delaying, Jena sighed in resignation.

"Tell his lordship I will be down as soon as I make myself more presentable," Jena said.

"I'll wait for you, ma'am. To show you the way, like," the girl explained, then suddenly remembering her further instructions, she thrust a can of hot water into Jena's hands.

Jena took the can and eased the door closed. She cupped her hands around the metal, grateful for the warmth that seeped into her skin. Smiling wanly at the worried expression on the old woman's face, she hurried to the commode. She washed her hands and face, then made a moue of despair at her reflection in the mirror. Wisps of black hair straggled from her disordered braid. Finding her reticule, she rummaged for her brush and untangled the plait, brushing vigorously until her hair crackled. Hastily she tied it at the back of her neck and once more crossed to the bed.

"Don't look so worried," she whispered, leaning over to kiss Nanny's wrinkled cheek. "Everything will turn out fine."

Jena followed the maid, who kept casting nervous glances over her shoulder as though she were afraid the strange young woman might somehow get lost in the multitude of corridors. Jena was impressed by the quiet opulence of the rooms through which they passed. Apparently the viscount had no lack of funds, and more taste than wit. The housemaid led her down an enormous sweeping staircase and opened the door leading to a brightly lit, cheerful room.

Jena stood in the doorway transfixed by the sight of Lord Devereaux Havenhurst, her husband. She sighed in relief, thankful that her memory had not been faulty. Although she suspected that she had seen him at his worst, in the morning light, cleanly shaven and dressed, her husband was an extremely good-looking man.

There were dark circles beneath his blue eyes, but little evidence of the hangover that should have been apparent. Jena winced at the red weals marking his cheek, where her nails had scratched him during the kidnapping. His white hair shone like a beacon in the dark-wooded room, a sharp contrast to his youthful good looks. Jena kept her eyes focused on his hair as she crossed the parquet floor to the chair being held by an impassive footman. She sank gratefully into the seat and dropped her eyes to stare at the pristine linen tablecloth. She waited as the servant's gloved hand placed a gold-rimmed china plate heaped with food before her. Only when a cup of tea was set beside her hand did her eyes move to the face of the man opposite her.

Despite the scratches, her husband's handsome face held no hostility. Encouraged slightly, she reached out a shaking hand for the cup of tea. She slowly raised the cup to her lips, keeping her gaze steady on the man. She refused to be intimidated until she could gauge his reactions to their impossible situation. Dev smiled thinly, but his eyes remained untouched by emotion. With a flick of his wrist, he signaled for the servants to leave the room. The silence seemed oppressive to Jena, but she refused to be the first to speak.

"I trust you slept well, madam."

The quietly spoken social comment almost sent Jena into an attack of the giggles. She fought down her nervous reaction and answered briefly. "Yes, thank you."

"Perhaps after you have had something to eat, we might remove to the library for a discussion of our predicament."

Jena looked hopelessly at the heaping plate in front of her and wondered if she dared eat any of the food. Her stomach was fluttering so much with nervousness that she was afraid to touch anything but a slice of toast. Dev appeared completely relaxed—although, with the way his fork rose and fell with such constant regularity, Jena wondered if he actually tasted anything. It was as though he was determined to eat everything on his plate only because his body required it. Silently Jena finished her toast, took a last sustaining swallow of tea, and folded her hands in her lap. As though waiting for this signal, Dev rose and walked around to her side.

Gulping nervously, Jena jumped up and followed him as he led the way across the foyer.

The library looked different in the morning brightness. The hurried marriage ceremony performed in the candlelit room was only a memory. Dev strode behind the carved mahogany desk, waiting for her to be seated before he lowered himself into the high-backed leather chair. He stared across at Jena, opened his mouth to speak, then closed it as he pushed a hand through his white hair. Then he shook his head, eyeing her with embarrassment.

"I don't know your name." The words burst from him, sounding harsh in the silent room.

"It's Jena. Jena Christie." Her own lips were stiff with the awkwardness of the situation. She pressed herself against the wooden back of her chair, trying to ease her ragged breathing.

"This is a damnable affair, Jena." Dev slapped his hand on the surface of the desk in exasperation. "We have to find an equitable solution to this contretemps."

"I'm sorry," Jena mumbled.

"It's not your fault, my dear," Dev said magnanimously. "My friends and I were castaway when we arrived at this wonderful idea for my marriage. You are in no way to blame. I take full responsibility for my actions."

Jena was grateful that the viscount could view the situation with such equanimity. Someone less gentlemanly might be furious and lay the entire fiasco at her door. Not that she felt guiltless. She had made her own decision last night and accepted the viscount's proposal, so she must be prepared to accept some responsibility for their predicament.

But she was thankful that her new husband seemed to be so reasonable.

Dev, hands steepled beneath his chin, stared intently at the polished surface of the desk. His eyes were unfocused, his mind intent on an examination of the night before.

Grateful for a chance to study her new husband, Jena let her eyes wander freely over his person. Her heart lurched at the handsome figure he made. She might have been in worse circumstances. He was undeniably good-looking, and perhaps once they got to know each other they might find a measure of happiness in their unorthodox union. She empathized with the awkwardness of his situation. But he seemed rational, and she hoped that he would permit her some time to get used to him before he required any additional duties. She suspected that, once acquainted with Dev, she might not find her marital obligations particularly onerous. As her eyes once more slid over his chest, she blushed at her own boldness.

"Well, down to business, my girl," Dev said, breaking into Jena's thoughts. "I certainly don't wish to be unreasonable. I am prepared to offer you a sizable settlement in return for the annulment. Thank God, the marriage was never consummated!" he exclaimed less than tactfully. "We should have little trouble. I will explain it all to my man of business. He will of course handle all of the details."

At first Jena thought she had misunderstood him, yet as he continued on to mention various sums and lawyers, the horror of her situation became abundantly clear. It had never occurred to her that he would inveigh against the marriage. For a moment the room spun and Jena panicked at the thought she might swoon at the odious man's feet. Then anger rescued her and she narrowed her eyes at the man across the desk. How could she ever have considered him a gentleman? She had even been feeling sorry for him!

"No!" Jena said, then halted, further angered by the flash of astonishment in the viscount's eyes. It was as though an inanimate object had broken into his train of thought.

"No?" Dev repeated, cocking his head as though he had misunderstood her. His blue eyes stared coldly at the girl, noting the high color splashed across her cheekbones in an otherwise pale face. "To exactly what part of the plan do you object, my dear?"

"To all of it," Jena blurted out. "An annulment is quite impossible."

"Ah ha." Dev let his breath out in a sharp hiss. Once more he was about to see the avaricious nature of women. Luckily, he had few illusions left concerning the gentle sex. He sighed, knowing that last night's disaster was going to be extremely expensive, but wanting only to end the degrading negotiating and discover the price for his idiocy. "Perhaps you might enlighten me as to the exact nature of your desires. I'm sure we can come to some equitable agreement."

Jena ignored the sarcastic tone of Dev's voice. She remembered to her shame liking the deep timbre, even though he had been well under the hatches when he spoke his commitment to their marriage. Quickly she brought her wandering thoughts back to the discussion at hand. She must remain calm. She had been coldly rational when she'd agreed to the wedding, and nothing had changed since that time. Except that the man she had married was an arrogant boor.

"I cannot agree to the annulment." Jena faltered

54

as Dev's blue eyes took on a flinty cast. "Whether the marriage was consummated or not"—Jena flushed red with embarrassment at such plain speaking—"is beside the point. The ceremony was incontestably legal. Your friends were present, your servants are aware of the situation, and you were not coerced. It would be impossible to keep last night a secret. My virtue would be forever questioned and my reputation destroyed. Therefore I cannot agree to the annulment."

A sharp bark of laughter shattered the quiet of the room. Dev stared across at the bristling girl, marveling at her ability to portray "innocence abused" with such accuracy. If he hadn't known better, he could almost believe that the beautiful actress was outraged at the slur on her character. His eyes glittered as he cataloged her attributes, determining instantly that once they finished haggling over the price, he would set her up as his mistress. Despite her audacity, or maybe even because of it, he was drawn to the girl. He had the feeling she would not bore him as quickly as had the others before her.

"You're coming it a bit too brown," Dev drawled, his eyes once more dropping to the softly rounded figure beneath the unfashionable dress. "Name your price and let's have done with this farce, my girl."

"I am not 'your girl' and I have no intention of being, you pompous beast," Jena snapped. She found herself panting in her agitation, wanting nothing so much as to slap the smug smile off the man's face. "I have no price, as you so boorishly suggest. I realize that this is an appalling situation. I am more than willing to make some concession to your anger at the irregularity of it all. However, I refuse to accept your insinuations that

I am here to wrest some sort of personal gain from the situation."

"I may have been drunk as a lord last night, my dear," Dev ground out. "But I am not a wet-behind-the-ears nodcock eager to be taken in by some wide-eyed, soft-spoken Cyprian."

"How dare you, sirrah!"

Jena leaped to her feet, fury blinding her to her own actions. Her fists opened and closed in frustration, and without conscious thought she grasped the vase of flowers in front of Dev. She was suddenly assailed by the memory of the dripping roses of her wedding bouquet and she raised the vase over her head and deliberately smashed it in the very center of the desk.

There was absolute silence in the room except for the muted dripping of water onto the Aubusson carpet. The red nail scratches stood out starkly against Dev's otherwise expressionless face. He had not moved so much as an eyebrow. Coldly, he surveyed the mass of broken pottery, sodden papers, and mangled flowers.

Absolutely appalled at her total loss of control, Jena fell back in her chair and covered her face with her hands. Her whole body trembled in reaction to her outrageous behavior.

"Crying has absolutely no effect on me," Dev snapped, his eyes narrowed at the affected picture of despair. He was not surprised when the cheeky girl raised her head and glared at him from tearless gray eyes. He had weathered several stormy scenes with cast-off mistresses, and he knew all the tricks of this girl's profession.

"I'm terribly sorry that I lost my temper," Jena apologized.

Dev liked the slight musical tone of her low voice and was impressed with the air of quality that pervaded the girl's behavior. Once they reached an agreement he was more than ever convinced she would make an exciting lover. He smiled at her primly brushed hair, wondering how it would look loosed and tumbled in riotous curls across a pillow. Then, as she continued speaking, his heart hardened at the words.

"I have explained that I cannot agree to an annulment. My name and reputation would be ruined. The marriage is legal, and somehow we shall have to make the best of it," Jena finished quietly.

Anger such as Dev had never known coursed through his body at the finality of the actress's voice. He had seen many greedy women in his lifetime, but this prim-faced tart was the outside of enough. He would be eternally damned before he would give in to such blackmail. Dev cleared the desktop with one savage swipe of his arm, satisfied as the girl's body jerked in fear. Her wide gray eyes raised to his and he held her glance with determination.

"Devil take it, madam! You try my patience," he said through clenched teeth. He glared across the desk at the girl, amazed that she didn't flinch as his eyes flashed fire. "You are an actress I picked up in an alleyway. You have neither name nor reputation to be concerned with. I will not be badgered any longer! I tell you now that there is no power on this earth that would force me to remain married to you."

Chapter Five

Dev and Jena glared across the desk, each one refusing to break the duel of glances. A hesitant scratching at the door interrupted their concentrated anger.

"Come," Dev snarled.

Although Jena suspected the entire household must be aware of the argument taking place in the library, there was not the slightest bit of curiosity on the face of the starched butler who entered. Chambers's round face was bland as he faced the viscount. Not an eyelash flickered at the jumble of pottery, flowers, and water littering the floor beside the desk.

"The Duke of Wayfield's carriage is just arriving, milord," Chambers intoned in sepulchral tones.

"Good God! Grandfather!" Dev leaped to his feet, starting to follow the servant toward the door. Suddenly he ground to a halt and swung around to face Jena. "You've got to get out of here."

"Milord?" The butler turned, his face puckered in bewilderment.

"Not you, Chambers," Dev snapped, pointing an accusatory finger at the startled figure in the chair. "Her!"

Jena drew herself up, prepared to do battle at

this further example of her husband's insulting behavior. "I beg your pardon!"

"Another time, if you please, madam," Dev said, too distracted to hear the outrage in her voice. "For the nonce, let it suffice to say our adieus. Chambers, show this person a room where she can wait."

"But, Lord Havenhurst, she . . . I mean, you . . ." The flustered butler was clearly losing his hardfought control.

"No need to cry craven," Dev said, biting off each word. "Go do the pretty with the duke and I'll get the young lady settled in the dungeons."

"But, milord, we don't have—"

"Get out!" Dev roared, advancing on the wide-eyed girl as the butler bolted from the room.

As he strode toward her, Jena sprang out of her chair and began backing across the room. Dev quickened his pace and reached out to grasp her arm, but Jena batted his hand away. At any other time the look of injured surprise on her husband's face might have amused her, but now it only further enraged her.

"You've got to get out. I'll deal with you later," Dev hissed, casting a harried look over his shoulder.

"I'm not leaving!" Jena cried. Although the thought of further insults thrown by the viscount was terrifying, she had no intention of quitting the field. She had stupidly entered into this marriage and she had to convince him that he would have to try to make a go of it. She must make Lord Havenhurst understand that she was not being stubborn but that she had no other alternative.

"If you refuse to leave, I will tell my grandfather the entire sordid story and you will end up with nothing. The duke will never permit such a scandal to become the *on dit* of the century. I can hear the

59

old tabbies now discussing how an encroaching actress tried to force the heir to the Duke of Wayfield into a sham marriage." Dev's voice, though low, lashed out at Jena.

Far from intimidated by the furious viscount, Jena felt consumed by righteous anger. Forgotten were any kindly feelings toward the handsome gentleman. Gone was her understanding of his dismay at their situation. All fled in the rush of indignation that flooded her at his contemptuous accusations. How dare he try to wiggle out of this marriage just because he thought she was an actress! It should make no difference if she were lady or lightskirt. He had entered into this marriage, and now, just because he felt she was socially inferior, he wanted to escape the results of his actions. Never! Jena vowed.

"I'm staying," Jena announced, sweeping around the dumbfounded viscount. She stalked to the marble fireplace and flounced down into the wing chair drawn close to the briskly crackling fire. Once seated, some of the hauteur that had given her courage fled and she huddled against the embroidered cushions waiting for an explosion from her husband. Before this could take place, the door once more opened.

Jena caught her breath at the impressive figure framed in the doorway. The Duke of Wayfield was as tall as Dev but slighter of build. However, the resemblance of the two men was marked. The seventy-year-old man had the same white head of hair and the same disdainful look of arrogance etched deeply into his face. His hawk nose jutted out over a mouth drawn tight with displeasure as his faded blue eyes scanned the room to settle on Dev.

"Well, Devereaux, what have you to say for yourself?" the duke snapped. Although his voice was slightly quavery, there was no hint of weakness in the tone. "What freakish start are you up to now, that you must set that dithering Chambers to bar your door?"

"Good morning, Grandfather. You must have left Wayfield before the cock finished crowing," Dev said. He leaned negligently against the mantelpiece, the picture of the city gentleman comfortably at home.

Although the duke had not looked directly at Jena, she knew he had seen her where she cowered in the chair. For an instant she wished that she had left the room, because she did not relish the coming interview under the predatory gaze of the old man. She suspected there was not the slightest detail in the room the man had not already scrutinized.

"A dash early to be entertaining, Dev," the duke said, indicating with a raised eyebrow the girl in the chair.

The duke walked stiffly forward until he stood directly in front of Jena. Nervously she rose from the chair and bobbed a curtsy as Dev rattled off cursory introductions.

"This is Jena, Your Grace," Dev drawled insultingly. "My grandfather. The Duke of Wayfield."

Jena flushed with embarrassment as the duke's sharp eyes took in her disheveled dress and her unbound hair. Her eyes faltered at his steady gaze and she sank back into the chair, her body trembling at the awkwardness of her position.

Chambers's entrance broke the tension of the three figures beside the fire. Time was spent settling the duke in the chair opposite Jena. When tea was offered she grasped at the cup, grateful for the opportunity to focus on anything other than the scene in the library. With all her heart she wished that she had bolted before the duke's entrance. Her mind was whirling with the events of last night and this morning. She had been kidnapped, married, deserted on her wedding night, and now her husband was refusing to acknowledge their marriage. She wanted nothing more than to push the time back and begin yesterday all over.

If there were only herself to consider, Jena would have taken great pleasure in ripping the ring from her finger and throwing it at the feet of the arrogant viscount. But there was Nanny to think of and all of the others at the home farm. She knew she had been wrong to agree to the marriage for security. Last night she had been tired and desperate, and now her situation was even worse.

"Perhaps, Devereaux, you would care to enlighten me as to your relationship with this young person."

The softly spoken words brought a flush of heat to Jena's cheeks which did not go unnoticed by the duke. He doubted if there was a bark of frailty in all of London who could still conjure up a blush. The situation was still more curious because, despite the deplorable wardrobe of the chit, she had a definite look of quality. His face politely curious, the duke cocked his head at his grandson, waiting for the young man to speak.

"We are married," Jena said into the tense silence.

She flinched as both men's eyes swung to her, one pair flashing with fury, the other pair wide with shock. The spoken words eased the terror that had been building inside her. Suddenly she was calm. The blurted announcement was all she was able to articulate. Now all she could do was to wait for the reactions of the two men. Dev's explosion was not long in coming.

"We are not married!" Dev's voice was harsh

with controlled animosity. He glared down at Jena, wanting nothing more than to strangle the infuriating tart. He could almost feel his hands around her slender throat, tightening around her white skin. Her smoky gray eyes would widen as she clung to him, begging for release. He could imagine her soft bosom rising and falling in her distress. "Damn!"

Dev pushed himself away from the mantel, pacing across the carpet in his agitation. Devil take it, he raged. The girl had taken possession of him. How could he be furious with her one minute and wanting to make love to her in the midst of it all? The sooner he thrust her out of his life, the happier he would be. Deciding thus, he felt more in control of the situation. He turned and stalked back to the fireplace. Ignoring the black-haired temptress completely, he spoke directly to his grandfather.

"I'm sorry to admit, Your Grace, that I have acted like a perfect idiot. Last evening I had more brandy than was wise and have landed myself in the briars. I'm sorry if any of this causes you discomfort, but I believe I can handle the situation."

Jena marveled at the tone of voice of the man she had known for such a short time. It presented another side to the contrary viscount. He spoke man to man with the duke, neither asking forgiveness nor offering excuses. He was merely stating facts. Jena had seen anger, ridicule, arrogance, charm, and foolish drunkenness. But now she saw a mature gentleman who was confident enough to need no apologies. In such a few words Dev communicated honesty, sincerity, and a great deal of warmth. However, his next words totally negated any softening of Jena's judgment of Dev's character.

"The young lady is an actress I scooped off the

street last night. After an evening of revelry with some friends, it seemed perfectly logical to marry the girl. When you arrived we were negotiating for a proper settlement of the affair." Dev spoke concisely, never once looking in Jena's direction.

The duke, although giving attention to his grandson, was fully aware of the reactions of the girl in the chair. At Dev's first words, she blanched, her skin taking on an almost translucent appearance. Her gray eyes had the look of a wounded animal, but as Dev continued to speak there was a flash of fire in the suddenly narrowed gaze. Gad, but the girl was a beauty! Here was no namby-pamby, prinked-out deb, full of airs and caprices. The duke was fascinated by the situation. He had seldom seen Dev at a disadvantage, but his grandson appeared flustered by the lovely girl.

"I gather you were having some difficulty arriving at terms," the duke said, glancing pointedly at the broken vase beside the desk. He took in the flash of irritation in his grandson's eyes but was far more impressed by the squirm of embarrassment of the young woman. Her reaction was one he might have expected from a well-bred gentlewoman, not a woman of loose morals. Behind his impassive expression, the duke's mind whirled with conjecture.

"Perhaps, Grandfather, you would prefer to retire to your room," Dev suggested, bringing the duke's attention back to the situation at hand. "I will finish my discussion with Jena, and then we can look in at White's."

It was none of the duke's intention to be cheated of any of the details of this affair. Aside from the bald statement of marriage, the girl had not spoken. The old man was anxious to hear the story of last night from her viewpoint.

"Well, young woman," the duke rasped out, making the girl jump in apprehension. "Let's have your story. And spare me your tears and blushes. There's a scandal broth brewing, and I mean to hear the right of it. No Banbury tales, if you please."

Jena's breath caught in her throat, and although she opened her mouth, she could utter no sound. She was aware of the ominous silence of the figure against the mantelpiece. It was this very awareness that brought a return of resentment at her misusage. Granted the entire idea had been fantastical. How ever it had been conceived, the marriage had taken place and she must make her husband realize the validity of their union. She realized that her only hope to regularize her situation was to convince the duke of her story.

"Your grandson is under the impression that I am no better than a lightskirt," Jena began, leaning forward in her chair and staring intently at the old man. "There is some justice to this belief as he did accost me outside a theater, but I was engaged in honest work. My name is Lady Jena Stacie Lynn Christie. My father was Sir George Christie of Dunton House."

Dev snorted in derision and Jena glared up at the man. Their eyes touched and she felt scorched by the heated glance that seemed to slide over her face and body. She could feel a flush rise in her cheeks, and she clenched her fists trying to control her anger.

The duke sank back against the cushions of his chair, jolted by this sudden turnabout. He had known Sir George Christie, having met him at various race meetings in his salad days. The man was a charming reprobate with a penchant for gambling. He could see little resemblance between the man he remembered slightly and the strikingly beautiful girl across from him. If the chit's story was true, it explained the air of breeding and quality about her. And it also changed the situation totally. The duke pursed his lips, controlling his expression to one of extreme disinterest. Only his eyes held a hint of cunning as he stared back and forth between his skeptical grandson and the indignant girl.

"Have you notified your father?" The duke wondered if he would next be subjected to an interview with a wrathful parent.

Jena's eyes came back to rest on the duke. "Both my parents are dead, Your Grace," Jena said.

"I see. Well, madam, I will accept your antecedents for the moment," the duke announced. "But I find it difficult to believe that any woman of breeding and sensibility would enter into a havey-cavey marriage with a man she had met on the street."

Jena blanched at the note of scorn in the old man's voice. She drew herself up and stared across at the formidable figure in the wing chair. Her voice was quietly controlled, almost colorless as she began to speak.

"I met your grandson last evening outside the theater where I am—eh—was employed."

"You are an actress?"

"Certainly not!" Jena had not missed the slight note of disdain in the duke's voice, nor the hint of skepticism that crept into his eyes. Fighting back her own anger, she continued more quietly. "No, Your Grace. My old nanny and I were working there as seamstresses."

Her nanny indeed! The duke was annoyed with himself for being taken in by the girl's innocent air. He had actually begun to believe her story. Parents dead. Working as a poor but honest seamstress. It had all the markings of a melodrama. But a nanny was carrying things too far. What a farrago of nonsense! "And might I inquire as to the whereabouts of your redoubtable chaperone?" he asked, his voice icy with sarcasm.

"When I came down for breakfast, she was still in the bedroom we shared last night."

Jena knew that she had shaken the duke, by the tightening of his jaw muscles and the narrowing of his eyes. Even though the old man quickly hooded the intensity of his gaze, the gleam of surprise gave her hope that she might convince him of her truthfulness.

"Continue, please." The duke rested his elbows on the arms of his chair, his tented fingers resting on his chest. His eyes never left the girl, searching out the nuances in her voice and her expression.

"Lord Havenhurst and his friends accosted us outside the theater."

"Accosted?"

"Your grandson was not himself, Your Grace," Jena said.

"Disguised?" the old man asked, his eyes sparkling despite the gravity of the situation.

"Castaway, at the very least," Jena answered demurely.

"There is no need to be so hesitant to blacken my character," Dev snapped. "I was quite odiously drunk, Grandfather."

"As you say, Lord Havenhurst," Jena said, nodding graciously in his direction. "Nanny and I were brought here after a slight struggle."

"Devereaux!" the duke roared. "That a grandson of mine should raise a hand to one of the gentler sex!"

"Gentler sex! Hah!" Pushed beyond his tolerance, Dev pointed a shaking finger at the livid scratches marring his white face. "That young woman tried to blind me. And her nanny! Don't picture any sweet-tempered, white-haired biddy. The harridan has a voice that could penetrate stone walls and a set of dabblers I'd put up against Gentleman Jackson himself."

"How dare you talk about Nanny that way, you great bully!" Jena leaped from her chair, her hair billowing away from her neck as she whirled to face her accuser. "Nanny was only trying to protect me. There you were, you four louts, pushing and threatening her. She's an old woman and she might have been hurt," Jena wailed, losing control at the sudden realization.

At the girl's outburst, Dev caught his breath, fascinated by her magnificence. Although he heard her voice, the words did not penetrate to his brain. He was wholly caught up in the magic of the moment. Jena blazed with the intensity of her fury. He could just imagine what she would look like in the raptures of passion. He moved toward her, then froze as her expression changed and her eyes filled with tears. For one moment he wanted to take her in his arms and comfort her, but then he remembered why that was so impossible.

"Spare me your tears," he said, the words cutting to remind himself that this was not time to show weakness.

Both combatants were oblivious to the duke's fascinated scrutiny. The old man missed none of the contrasting expressions that flitted across his grandson's face. Wonder, desire, distrust, were all there in ample doses. And the girl was not intimidated by the lad. No matter her parentage, there was backbone aplenty in her character.

Jena returned to her chair, taking a deep breath to regain control. If she hadn't been tired and upset, she would have never behaved so shrewishly. She closed her eyes for a moment and then once more faced the granite-jawed duke.

"I beg your pardon, Your Grace, for such an unseemly display of bad temper." She settled back in her chair and took up her narrative. Her words were precise, her tone remote. "When we arrived here, your grandson informed me that he intended to marry me. We tried to dissuade him, but he was adamant."

The sparsity of details gave the duke's imagination full play. His face darkened and his eyes were regretful as he looked at the carefully controlled expression of the girl across from him. There was a grace to her manner that pleased him and a practical streak evident in the noncommital statement of the facts.

"You were aware that my grandson had been drinking?"

"It was quite evident," Jena admitted. "I did not take advantage of his condition. Nanny and I, and even the vicar, tried to convince him to release me. However, he refused to consider any other option but marriage." She paused, taking a shaky breath. "And so in the end, Your Grace, I agreed to marry him. My own situation was such that I felt I must accept."

The duke waited, but the girl did not continue. He was curious as to the circumstances that forced her to take such a drastic step, but since she did not intend to explain, he would not badger her.

"Can't we get on with this, Grandfather?" Dev said, his temper flaring as he listened to the chit trying to put a good face on such a shabby affair. "I have already admitted my dishonorable role in this bogus event."

"Was the marriage legal?" the duke asked.

69

There was silence in the room, except for the occasional crackle from the logs in the fireplace. Dev pushed a hand through his hair, glaring down at Jena, who ducked her head, staring intently at the pattern on the carpet. She was anxious to hear his response. She could not tell how much of her story the duke believed, but suspected that if Dev denied the legality of her claim, she could put period to any hopes from that quarter.

"Max supplied me with a special license," Dev declared, his voice cracking at the admission. "Reggie's brother, the vicar, performed the ceremony."

"And I suppose that lummox Dickon served as your groomsman," the duke sneered. "I should have known those imps of Satan would be abetting your downfall."

"You are speaking of my friends, Grandfather," Dev said coldly.

"Hah!" the duke grunted. "A pretty picture, Devereaux! Four drunkards and a midnight wedding. A ramshackle affair, at best. How do you think this will be received by the gabble-mongers of the *ton*? Is there a one of those stiff-necked tabbies who will believe this hole-in-corner event? You'll be a laughingstock, sir!"

"Rather a laughingstock that a dupe," Dev drawled, smiling triumphantly at the wide-eyed girl in the chair. "Despite her outlandish claims, she is no better than she should be. I do not intend to be leg-shackled to an actress. I'll not accept this marriage, Grandfather. Think of the Wayfield line."

Jena held herself upright, refusing to show weakness by touching her back to the cushions of the chair. She felt the horror of her situation, but more than that, a deep-seated anger at the man who was her husband. How dare he dismiss anyone on the basis of class? How dare the abominable man ap-

peal to the tradition-bound duke using such an un-
fair argument? It was definitely war. And if he
could appeal to the old man's unimpeachable an-
cestry, so could she. She wished she had paid closer
attention to the actresses at the theater. She was
about to give the performance of her life and hoped
she could do the role justice.

"Oh yes, Your Grace, do think of the line." Jena's
voice sounded shrill to her own ears and she lowered her tone to an embarrassed whisper. "Even
now, I may be carrying the heir to the next gener-
ation of Wayfields."

"God in Heaven!" Dev swore in exasperation, his
eyes dazed at the audacity of the hussy. He charged
forward to tower in fury over the girl in the chair.

Jena had no need to feign agitation. She was terrified by Dev's belligerent figure. She fumbled in
her reticule until she found a handkerchief, bury-
ing her face in the concealing folds. She couldn't
bare to look at the man, appalled at the magnitude
of her lie.

It took all the control that the duke had not to
guffaw in the face of such an obvious fabrication.
He knew his grandson well, and the look of outraged innocence on Dev's face bespoke the truth of
the situation. As for the girl, he had caught the
look of desperation in her eyes and then the rise of
indignation at his grandson's less than tactful accusations. She had the goodness to be ashamed at
her own tactics, but the duke had no intention of
letting this heaven-sent opportunity pass.

He had wanted Devereaux to marry. Although he
would check the girl's story, he was prepared to
accept the fact that she was the daughter of Sir
George Christie. She had all of the markings of a
well-born lady. No matter the circumstances, as a
gentleman, Devereaux must honor his marriage.

"Enough," the duke said. His voice was quiet, but there was steel beneath the words.

Dev swung around, his face a shuttered mask. The girl peeked over the edge of her lacy handkerchief, her eyes great pools of apprehension. The duke ignored her, focusing his attention on his grandson.

"How much do the servants know of this shabby affair?" the duke asked abruptly.

"I would assume they know that the marriage was performed. We made little secret of the affair," Dev answered. His words were drawled, but there was a bleakness to his eyes. "They know nothing of the history of the girl or the method of our, uh, introduction. We did not see fit to enlighten the vicar, more's the pity, for then he would have been even more adamant against the ceremony."

For several minutes there was silence in the room. The duke considered all sides of the dicey situation. Satisfied at last, he nodded his head in one jerky motion. Slowly he pulled himself from the chair, facing the two young people. His eyebrows bunched over his hawk nose as he made his pronouncement.

"I am returning to Wayfield, but before I go I will place an announcement in the papers concerning this marriage." The duke raised his hand to forestall Dev's interruption. "The story that I am prepared to confirm is that your regard for the lady is of long standing. Naturally, I shall condemn the impetuosity of youth which drove you to such a precipitous step as a midnight wedding."

The duke took several stiff steps toward the door, aware of the almost palpable silence in his wake. He did not need to look at his grandson to feel the heated glance boring into his back. The young cock should know better than to try to outwit a vintage bird. The old man chuckled. At the doorway, he turned and drew himself erect. His bearing proclaimed him the Duke of Wayfield.

"I do not care what transpired before now," he said. "You two will have to work out some sort of suitable arrangement. Marriages have occurred in stranger circumstances, although at this moment I cannot think of one quite as exceptional as this. No matter. I expect you both to accept your idiocy with a reasonable amount of grace and find a way to deal together. For better or worse, you are married."

Chapter Six

Even after the door closed behind the duke, the room remained in the grip of a strained silence. Dev stood frozen in position, one hand raised in futile protest. Jena held her breath, her eyes steady on the closed portal, half-afraid the intimidating old man would return to deny his final words. She had won, but there was little joy in her triumph. Instead, a bitterness rose in her throat and she swallowed convulsively, forcing away the wave of fear that threatened to engulf her. Finally accepting the reality of the duke's departure, she relaxed against the padded chair back. Slowly her eyes swung to take in the ashen face of her husband.

The slight movement of the girl in the chair broke into Dev's glacial attitude. "Damn and blast!" he swore, with great feeling.

He swung around, facing the mantel, his hands gripping the wooden edge, white-knuckled from the emotional pressure he was trying to contain. Jena felt the muscles of her neck tensing as she waited for the explosion. She did not flinch when Dev swung around, his face a mask of accusation.

"Now look what you've done!" he shouted.

"Look what *I've* done?" she squeaked, unable to

control her own temper. "You insufferable cad! This whole bloody thing is your fault."

Appalled at her own language, Jena clapped both hands to her mouth as if to prevent any further unladylike slips. Her expression was so shocked that for a moment the humor of their situation slipped through Dev's guard. He chuckled, and the mere action brought his own ragged thoughts back under control. He covered his face with his hands, rubbing his fingers wearily against the skin. Finally he dropped his hands and stared across at the girl, who was blinking rapidly at his abrupt change of humor. Without a word he pushed away from the mantel and flopped into the chair across from her.

"You're right, you know," Dev said with deceptive honesty. "This whole thing is my fault."

Jena squinted suspiciously at the viscount. She did not know what to make of his sudden about-face. A smile tugged at the corner of his mouth, and she found herself staring at the firm lips. There was a charm about the man that she found slightly daunting. She had been able to handle his anger and his arrogance, but she suspected that his engaging appeal was a far more dangerous trait. She would be a fool to trust him, she lectured herself.

"Perhaps we can admit an equal culpability," Jena suggested pacifically. "Fair is fair."

Slowly the good-humored expression faded and his forehead furrowed in remembered anger. "You can hardly cry fair when you have just told my grandfather, a duke of the realm, may I remind you, the most shameless lie. Heir to the Wayfield line indeed! I never touched you."

"Are you positive of that fact?" Jena asked coolly.

"Yes, my dear," Dev said in tones of complete conviction. "I am positive." His eyes followed the lines of her body, covering every inch, then returning to her mortified gaze. His voice was caustic when he spoke. "If I had made love to you, I would know it. I would be familiar with every curve and valley, every line and blemish. And I would see that knowledge in your eyes."

A wave of color flooded Jena's cheeks. She wriggled in an agony of embarrassment, unable to meet Dev's intense blue eyes. She could almost feel the heat from his gaze, burning through the protection of her clothing. She could not back down now. Only by concentrating on the desperation of her position was she able to turn a serene face to her husband.

"Your grandfather believes it to be true."

"Ah, yes. The Duke of Wayfield has spoken," Dev intoned in bitterness.

Jena's gaze lifted to the cold blue eyes of her husband. She did not shrink as he appeared to take her measure. She would not be intimidated. But as his eyes scanned her, she felt a curious weakness filtering through her body. She was, alternately, hot and cold. Although she did not drop her gaze, she shifted uncomfortably in her chair.

"And so, for better or worse, my dear, we are married," Dev said. "Lady Jena Havenhurst. It has a pleasing ring to it, don't you know."

"I was a lady before my marriage," Jena replied, her voice soft but precise.

Dev chose to ignore the double entendre. "Is this what you wanted? My title and wealth?" he asked

"You know it was not of my choosing," Jena said. She leaned forward in her chair, wanting to make Dev understand what had made her accede to his bizarre proposition. "I had little choice in the matter, Lord Havenhurst."

"Please, my dear, no lengthy defense of your actions. There is nothing that you can say that will convince me that you are a young girl fallen on

76

hard times. You might be able to bamboozle my grandfather, but acquit me of some little intelligence. I know what you are and I know what you want. Like all of your sisters before you, you have kept your eyes on the ultimate prize. Gold. It is amazing to me what women will do for it."

Jena would have thought that at this point she would be beyond anger. She had already borne more insults from this arrogant man than she could credit. But once more she felt the blood mounting to her cheeks and had to force herself to remain seated in the face of Dev's sneering accusations. It didn't matter what he thought she was. By his own grandfather's words, the marriage had been accepted. If she had only herself to consider, she would take great pleasure in cutting the man dead. But she was not a free agent; there were others depending on her. Bitterly she accepted the folly of her actions. She would not dignify his accusations with a defense.

"It appears we have reached a stalemate, Lord Havenhurst."

"I think not, my dear," Dev answered. "Before my grandfather interrupted, we were on our way to agreeing to some compatible solution. I am still open to negotiation."

"You are insulting, sir," Jena snapped. "The marriage must stand. My name and reputation are at stake."

"Ah, yes. Your name and reputation." Dev seemed unimpressed by this stumbling block. "And what about my name? And my reputation?"

"According to your grandfather, you have little of the latter to worry about," Jena said.

"Well done, my dear. A ready tongue indeed. But then I should have expected such a quick rejoinder from such a worthy opponent." Here Dev's eyes narrowed and he glowered at Jena. "It is war, my dear. You may think yourself extremely clever to have convinced my grandfather of your untarnished character, but I will never believe it. I do not want this marriage and I will do what I can to get out of it."

"But you can't!" Jena gasped.

"Would you care to bet on that fact?"

"No!"

Jena quailed at the arrested look in Dev's eyes. He had gone still, staring at her, although she sensed his mind was busy with some devious thoughts of his own. She did not know what he was thinking, but her suspicions were raised when she spotted the beginnings of a smile. Slowly the grin expanded, and the effect on her senses was more worrisome than whatever he was planning. His smile transformed Dev, giving a devilish cast to his eyes. Beware the wolf, she reminded herself.

"I have a proposition for you, my dear," Dev said, his voice softly cajoling.

"The last proposition you had for me was marriage," Jena snapped. "And now you're trying to weasel out of that."

Dev's smile dimmed for a second in a flash of anger. He knew he would get nowhere with the girl unless he could allay some of her suspicions. In all fairness, she had a right to her wariness. No matter who she was, he had treated her badly. He could not understand what it was about the black-haired temptress that brought out such knavish behavior. He had always been chivalrous in his relationships with women, but for some reason this beguiling wench forced him to actions that were beyond his ken. Never in his life had he treated a woman so unscrupulously. His very self-respect was at stake in his dealings with her.

"I realize, m'dear, that you have little faith in me," Dev began cautiously. "I have behaved badly, and for that I truly apologize. But I see no reason why we cannot come to some compromise that would be mutually satisfactory. Agreed?"

Jena examined Dev's bland expression, searching for the sincerity behind his words. She would not be lulled by fancy phrases. "I would like to think we might be able to work out something agreeable," she conceded.

"Excellent. Let's look at the facts. We have been married in a legally binding ceremony. My grandfather has accepted the marriage and will broadcast the event in London, mayhap even all of England in his joy at my capitulation to wedded bliss." Dev grinned engagingly to take the bite of sarcasm away from his words. "You have achieved the coup of the year by marrying the much-sought-after Viscount Badderley. Please don't bristle so. You must permit me some slight vanity in this case."

"I have only your word that maidens are swooning at your feet," Jena said dryly. She smiled sweetly as Dev's brows lowered at the set-down. "For the moment, I am prepared to accept the fact unchallenged."

"Graciously stated, madam," Dev observed. "To continue. Now that your situation is secure, through the support of my grandfather, it will become difficult for you to maintain your part of the bargain."

"What do you mean?" Jena asked, truly puzzled.

"Think on it. You could not possibly maintain the fiction that you are a fit wife for a viscount. Your acting ability aside, there are countless details that you would be unable to deal with. You would have an entire household to run, servants to hire and control, accounts to maintain. The day-to-day details are endless. Not to mention the social commitments. A young gentlewoman is schooled from the cradle to be able to take on the responsibilities of a titled husband. Years of specialized training are required. You may have been able to take on the outward veneer of a well-bred lady, but the obligations required are inborn, not learned in a day, a week, or a month."

Jena refused to rise to the bait at the man's insulting words. She knew he was hoping to force her into an untenable position so that she would cry craven, but he would be surprised at her own stubbornness. "Your point, milord?" she said, her voice showing only mild interest.

"I assume that you hope to rise in your fortunes through these unusual circumstances. You think marriage to me will benefit you socially and financially. What you have failed to take into consideration is that as my wife, you will receive only the allowance that I choose to give you. And if I should choose, I can put it about that I will not be responsible for any of your bills."

"You wouldn't dare!"

"You forget, my sweet." Dev's voice dripped sarcasm. "I do not desire this marriage. I will accept it only if I must, but I do not have to make it easy for you to fleece me."

Dev brought the full focus of his eyes to bear on Jena's infuriated figure. Although he fought to keep the blaze of passion well concealed, he knew she was aware of his interest by the rush of color to her cheeks.

"Perhaps you feel that your heightened social position will be worth the price. No theatrical training can have prepared you for the out-and-out snobbery of the servants. Once it becomes apparent that you are nothing more than a jumped-up actress, they will treat you with less respect than the lowest scullery maid. Society will take their cue from their servants, and you will find yourself a virtual pariah."

In the silence that followed his words, Dev leaned back in his chair, crossing his legs negligently as he stared morosely at the white-faced chit. He had to admit the girl had courage. Except for the ashen complexion, she appeared unmoved by the awful picture he had painted. He wished that he could see her eyes. Those expressive gray pools would give away her thoughts as surely as if she had spoken. But to his continued annoyance, she kept her eyes firmly fixed on the folded hands in her lap.

Jena could feel the tense knot of muscles across her shoulders. It had been such a long night, and now the morning seemed interminable. She was not sure how much longer she could continue to fight, but she was determined not to show any weakness. The viscount painted a bleak picture of her married life, except that he had no way of knowing that she had been outfitted to run a household and to take her place in society.

For years Jena had run Dunton House, acting as her father's hostess on the rare occasions when her father entertained. As she grew older and discovered the precarious state of her father's finances, she had taken over the accounts. Sometimes it had required all her ingenuity to juggle the bills so that they would not be left without credit. She had handled the books of the stud farm and the tenants as well. There was little she did not know about running an estate. Somehow she must use this unrevealed knowledge to thwart whatever plan Dev had in mind. She would have to be careful not to overplay her hand.

"I can play the part of a fine lady, guv." Jena bit her lip as if in consternation at the betraying slip of her tongue and ducked her head when she caught the gleam of triumph in her husband's eye.

"I'm quite sure you can, my dear," Dev purred. "But it would be such a strain. You'd have to worry every moment for fear of putting a foot wrong. And it's hardly necessary, when I am prepared to be generous. Granted, the duke will place the announcement in the newspapers, but it is possible to get a quiet annulment and leave here with your head high and your pockets well lined."

"No annulment," Jena stated clearly.

Dev cursed himself for moving too quickly. He schooled his face into placid lines as if he had expected just such a comment. Inwardly he raged at the stubborn wench. Despite the continued anger, he felt a flash of admiration for his worthy opponent. It had been a long time, if ever, that a woman had so exercised his mind. He would just have to return to his original scheme.

"You cannot carry off this masquerade," Dev sneered, delighted when the girl clenched her fists to keep control.

"I can, too!"

"Would you care to bet on that?" Dev asked. "Just a friendly wager between friends?"

"What do you mean?" The tremor in Jena's voice was real. She knew that the odious man was springing the trap he had been so carefully laying. This was the crucial test, and she hoped her mind was not too tired to be able to somehow outwit him.

"I would be willing to bet that you could not keep up appearances for three months."

"Don't patronize me, Lord Havenhurst. No wager is ever simple," Jena said. "Just exactly what will be the conditions of this wager."

Dev was surprised at the coolness of the girl. Then he realized that naturally she would be wholly practical. She was a business-woman and hoped to benefit substantially. How he hated greedy women. Angrily, he pushed himself out of the chair. Reluctant to observe the avaricious gleam within the wide gray eyes, he paced the carpet as he improvised.

"For my part, I will acknowledge the marriage. I will give you full authority over my household, the ability to hire and fire the servants, and an allowance for all expenses."

Jena considered the conditions, trying to foresee the possible pitfalls. She predicted no difficulties with the servants. From the little she had seen, both last night and this morning, the viscount's household ran like a well-oiled mechanism. Although Dev would not know it, she had enough experience and address to oversee the staff. Her point of dispute came in two areas: the allowance and Dev's acknowledgment.

"How much is the allowance?"

Dev named a figure that Jena suspected was far too low to run a house the size of the establishment she had seen. From what she had seen thus far of London, she knew everything was enormously expensive. Wages alone must be atrocious, and she knew he would cavil at any reduction of staff. She hated the thought of haggling, but Jena had no intention of losing this wager, so she must be pragmatic and look to her defenses.

"I assume you wish me to dress according to rank. As you can see, my clothes are inappropriate for the role. Since it must cover an entire wardrobe, the allowance is not large enough," Jena stated coolly.

How enterprising of the greedy little baggage to gain a new wardrobe from the situation. He should have foreseen that possibility, but then he suspected this might fall under the category of "the wages of sin." Dev had been expecting her to try to up the price, therefore, he was willing to negotiate. After several figures were suggested and rejected, they came to an acceptable total.

"Anything else, milady?" he sneered.

"You said you would acknowledge the marriage." Dev nodded his head mockingly and Jena continued. "I am fully aware that, with a jaundiced look or a few well-placed hints, you can utterly sink me in society. If that is your plan, the wager is pointless."

Now it was Dev's turn to shift uncomfortably. He had to admit the idea had occurred to him. It needed only a word from him that he had been tricked into the marriage, and the *ton* would give the girl the cut direct. The main disadvantage to the idea was that he would look the perfect fool. There was enough truth in the chit's surmise that Dev was eager to make amends.

"That would not be the act of a gentleman," Dev said in offended tones. "I will say or do nothing to indicate that I am other than overjoyed with my blushing bride. And to convince you of my good faith, I am prepared to be magnanimous. I realize it will take you some time to acclimate yourself to your new, shall we say, role. Therefore, I will put it about in the proper circles that we are not receiving while we explore the joys and novelties of wedded bliss."

Jena ground her teeth at his sarcastic tone, determined not to lose her temper again. "How long?" she snapped.

"What say you to a month?" Dev asked. "No doubt a bridegroom would be properly sated in that time."

His eyes glittered dangerously and Jena was reminded of the risk she was taking in trusting him.

"I must place a further condition to this wager," Jena announced. "Since the object of your gamble is to secure an annulment, there can be no question of any, um, marital privileges between us."

At Dev's raised eyebrow, Jena flushed to the roots of her hair. She wished he wouldn't look so amused at her discomfort. If she were to accept this infamous wager, she must protect herself from any unwelcome advances. Peeking through her lashes at the elegantly lolling figure of her husband, she wondered just how unwelcome his advances would be. Appalled at her wanton thoughts, Jena pulled herself straighter in her chair and faced Dev squarely.

"Although I find myself curiously reluctant to accept such a condition," Dev said, "I promise not to foist my attentions upon your virtuous person. Instead, I will offer prayers daily that you might reconsider."

"You will beggar yourself on votive candles before that will happen," Jena snapped.

"Methinks, m'dear, penury might be preferable to celibacy," Dev drawled.

Jena ignored the crudity, tilting her chin defiantly at Dev's chuckle of amusement. "And the terms of the wager?"

"I suspect you will not be able to sustain the fiction above a week, but I will be munificent and allow a full three months. In that time you must maintain my household as befits a viscount without going beyond your allowance. If for any reason you fail to fulfill your obligations, you will agree to an annulment."

"And if I win the wager?" Jena asked.

"In that unlikely event, my dear, I will honor the marriage contract."

Dev's final words seemed to reverberate off the book-lined walls of the library. Jena was careful not to show the slightest trace of triumph. She permitted her husband to gloat over the clever trap that he had laid for her. He thought that he had created an impossible scenario, the perfect wager. But the arrogant viscount had sorely underestimated the opposition. Jena had no intention of losing the wager. She needed the security that only marriage could give her.

Jena had been raised to believe she would marry someone of her father's choosing. She had been taught that love and personal happiness had little to do with the marital state. Perhaps Jena had acted precipitately, even foolishly, in marrying Lord Havenhurst. She was willing to accept the blame for her actions. However, the marriage was fact, and she could do nothing but fight for her rights. She would fight to win Dev's acceptance of the marriage. She would fight to save her name and reputation. But more than that, she would fight for the security of Nanny and all the others who depended on her.

"Well, my dear, have you considered the proposition?"

Dev's voice broke into Jena's thoughts and she quickly raised her eyes to his. In a now familiar reaction to her husband's gaze, her nerves tightened in an exhilarating manner. "I have, milord," she answered in a voice low but firm.

"Will you accept the wager?"

"I will."

Aware of the importance of her decision, Jena pushed herself to her feet. Dev uncoiled his long legs and rose to stand facing her. His size was in-

timidating and she trembled slightly at his closeness. He radiated danger, like a tiger ready to
spring. She flinched when he extended his hand to
seal the bargain.

"Word of a Wayfield, Lady Havenhurst," Dev intoned, clasping her soft hand and imprisoning it
within his own.

"Word of a Christie, Lord Havenhurst," Jena re-
sponded.

Jena caught the hint of triumph in the viscount's
blue eyes. She gritted her teeth to control her fury.
She supposed it would be undignified to kick him,
but the urge was overpowering. What a boor! she
railed. He thought he was so clever, but she would
show him. She'd win the wager; just see if she
didn't.

Chapter Seven

"That miserable, churlish, deceitful, unprincipled bounder!" Jena raged. She flung back the bedcovers, stamping her feet on the carpet in an excess of emotion. Contemptuously, she glared at the letter she had found on her breakfast tray. In a passion of frustration she crumpled the vellum, hurling it onto the eiderdown as if it were some loathsome vermin.

"Bad news, dearie?"

Nanny's mild question staggered Jena, and she swung around to face the woman in disbelief. The wrinkled face beneath the lacy mobcap was blank of expression, but the eyes were bright with intelligence. The sheer understatement in the question deflated Jena's burgeoning anger as nothing else could have, and she expelled her breath in a shaky sigh.

"Thank you, Nanny," Jena said, pushing the tumbled curls away from her face. "You always did know how to head off a temper tantrum."

"Anger blinds the wise man," Nanny stated solemnly. "A letter from the viscount?"

"Yes, the perfidious blackguard!" Jena was more rational now, but her fury was still clearly dominant. "I should have suspected that charming act he put on last evening was just to lull me into trusting him. Chatting through dinner and taking me on a tour of the house. All part of his devious plot."

"I warned you, Miss Jena, that the viscount would not make it easy for you to win the wager."

Jena had told her old friend of all that had transpired in the fateful interview with the Duke of Wayfield, and the wager she had contracted with her husband. Perhaps she had been smug in her own ability to win, but she had never expected such underhanded scheming by the man.

"Just listen to this, Nanny." With shaking fingers, Jena smoothed the paper across her knee, staring in fury at the flowing script. "He informs me that he knows I will want to manage my own household, so he has sent the servants to his other estates in order that I might hire a staff that I feel would be loyal to me. Since it may require several days to secure new servants, he has taken himself off to his shooting box for the week, so that I will not feel he is inconvenienced by the change of personnel. The bloody rotter!" Jena finished with feeling.

"Miss Jena!" Nanny scolded. "A lady should never give vent to such uncontrolled language."

"Fustian! A lady was never married to Lord Havenhurst."

"You'll have to admit, child, that it's a clever ploy."

Nanny continued to straighten the room, ignoring the dismay on the young girl's face. Jena's eyes followed the old woman, but her mind was busy as she pondered the implications of Dev's latest move. Her old friend was correct, she admitted grudgingly. His dismissal of the servants was cunning indeed. His staff might have accepted her blindly for the sake of the family name. Newly hired servants would need to be won over, and even then would scarce work as a loyal unit. In order to keep her part of the bargain, she would be forced to pay pricey wages for top-level help. With her limited finances that would be an impossibility.

"Checkmate in one move," Jena moaned.

"Will you let the viscount win so easily?"

Nanny's voice floated disembodied from the open dressing room door. So sunk in the sullens was Jena that for a moment she really did not hear the words. Then slowly, as the import of each syllable seeped into her brain, a resolution born of fury formed in her breast. Where was her backbone? She would not give the man the satisfaction of winning with such ease. She had promised herself she would win the wager, and by all that she held sacred, she would keep that promise.

"The Gray Fox will cry quits before I'm done!" Jena resolved.

Now that her fury had abated to a reasonable level, she was able to think more clearly. She moved the breakfast tray onto the bed and began to eat. She was unaware of the food, her mind busy with the magnitude of problems she faced. Using all the experience from juggling her father's accounts, she was confident she could run the viscount's smaller establishment. She even had the glimmer of an idea for hiring an adequate staff. There was a good possibility that she could win the wager. But in light of the underhanded methods of the viscount, she must come to terms with the future in the event that she lost.

Since her father's death, Jena had been fighting a losing battle of retrenchment. She had tried strict economies, but finally she had been compelled to break up the stud. Leasing Dunton House and her move to London had led her further down the path to eventual ruin. She had been forced to each step, controlled by the desperation of her circumstances. In order to survive she must take charge of her life. If she lost the wager, she would have only the lease money, a tarnished reputation, and the inevitable slide into the *demi monde*. Her father, although unable to do it himself, had always cautioned her to cover her bets.

Jena wiped her mouth with the linen napkin. She must contrive to win the wager and at the same time discover some way out of the morass of financial disintegration. Her only safety lay in her ability to build a future, with or without the viscount. Slowly a vision formed in her mind. On the surface, reopening the stud seemed a mere flight of fancy. On closer examination, Jena thought the idea might have distinct possibilities. The sheer audacity of the project fair took her breath away. Practical details whirled in her head and she was overcome by the hopelessness of it all.

Nanny was silent as she assisted her charge in her ablutions and then into her only dress. By the closed expression on Jena's face she knew the girl was deep in thought, and kept her own actions quiet and contained. She knew instantly when Jena had come up with a solution, because the girl froze in place, a startled look in her eye and a slow smile stretching her tightly pursed mouth.

"Martine."

Jena sighed as she uttered the single name. Martine Karac had been head groom of her father's stud farm. Gypsy blood ran heavy in his veins, giving him a magic touch with the most cantankerous horseflesh. That, combined with French thrift and practicality, made him the perfect answer to her prayers. If anyone could make her dream into a reality, it was Martine.

91

Suddenly Jena gurgled with laughter at a vivid remembrance of the old gypsy. Just before her sixth birthday she had confided to Martine that she wanted a horse of her own. He had told her to come to the stable at first light and he would have a surprise for her. Morning was only a promise when she hurried across the yard to be met by a line of solemn stable boys. With great ceremony they placed her atop a stack of hay bales. Heart pounding with anticipation, Jena waited.

The stable doors were flung open and a pantomime horse clattered across the cobblestones to where the wide-eyed child sat enthroned. The brown painted spots stood out sharply against the beige homespun costume. The head mask portrayed a noble beast with nostrils flared and teeth bared in a ferocious grimace. While Jena clapped in ecstasy, the horse, dipping and shaking its head, capered across the yard. There was no music for the dance, but for the child and the old man, the bond of their friendship provided the melody. Her father had given her a real horse for her sixth birthday, Jena remembered, but Martine's dancing horse would always be first in her heart.

"Have you any idea where Martine is working, Nanny?"

"Last I heard, he wasna working," the old woman said grimly.

"Nonsense. When he left, he said he was going to Lord Bayerly in Derbyshire."

"That was then. This is now. Word was there'd been an accident."

"He was hurt? And no one told me," Jena accused.

"Was nothing you could do, Miss Jena. The man would never take charity. He lost a leg," Nanny finished bluntly.

Jena shut her eyes in agony. A vision of the spry, cocky groom wavered in the quick tears that rose to her eyes. A stableman would be sorely handicapped, nay useless, without the agility of both legs. But Jena didn't need the man for his legs. She needed his head, his knowledge, and his experience.

"We'll start at Epsom," Jena announced briskly. "The trainers will know."

Despite Nanny's grumbling that a lady would never venture out to a common racecourse, Jena was adamant. She walked down the central staircase, her steps echoing hollowly in the empty house. Her mouth was pursed angrily as she checked each room, but the viscount had been true to his letter. Not a servant remained.

Their first stop was at Mistress McGuire's boardinghouse, where the two women packed their meager belongings. Jena removed her hoarded cache of coins from beneath a loose floorboard. The weight of her purse encouraged her, and briskly she dealt with her landlady. Ignoring the suggestive gleam in the woman's eye, Jena arranged for the delivery of their trunks. Without a backward glance, she bundled Nanny into a hackney and set out for Epsom.

Jena was slightly apprehensive about going to the racecourse. In her younger days she had accompanied her father to all the courses. But, she reminded herself, she had been dressed as a boy. The behind-the-scenes world of trainers, stable hands, and touts was definitely not the place for a lady. Ruefully she examined her brown dress, much the worse for three days' wear. She definitely did not look the part of a lady. Now was not the time for missish behavior. It mattered little whether she resembled a lady or a strumpet. Her first priority was to find Martine.

The hackney driver deposited them beside the stable compound. At Nanny's sharp reminder, Jena pulled her hat veil over her face. Then swallowing nervously, she straightened her spine and strode purposefully toward the doorway. No one barred their entrance, and Jena breathed in the familiar earthy scents with heightened pleasure. Her eyes scanned the faces of the scurrying figures until one certain face brought a smile to her lips. Her half boots clicked on the floorboards as she approached the young man stirring a bucket of mash.

"Timothy?"

"Aye, yuh," the lad said, jumping awkwardly upright when he beheld the two women.

"Is that any way to greet an old friend?" Jena lifted the veil, throwing it back in amusement as the boy's eyes lighted with recognition.

"Cooee! Miss Jena!" His eyes moved beyond her to the old woman standing quietly in the background. "And Nanny Ginthner."

"How are you, Tim?" Jena extended her gloved hand and the boy took it gingerly after wiping his own against the side of his overalls. "Do you work here or for one of the owners?"

"Here, Miss Jena. Worse the luck." Tim was a fine young man. He was not tall but had the lanky build of a colt, with whipcord muscles in his arms and legs. A mass of curly black hair covered his head, and his tanned face, though set in sober lines, was handsomely featured.

"Wages poor?"

"That and the runnin' of the place. Not what I'm used to," Tim sniffed. He had loved working for Sir George Christie and still mourned the breakup of the stud. "What do ye here, Miss Jena?"

"I need Martine," Jena answered quietly.

Tim's face took on a shuttered look at her question. Uneasily he glanced around, his feet shuffling in the straw on the floor. Jena waited with no sign of impatience, although she could feel her body tighten with the anxiety. Finally Tim moved away from her, picking up a rake without meeting her eyes.

"I could get a message to 'im," the boy mumbled.

Jena cursed the male conspiracy which on every level of society protected the womenfolk from unpleasantness. She knew half measures would not succeed. Any message that she left would remain unanswered.

"Don't be a sapskull, Timothy Leary!" Jena snapped, her voice low but steely in its fury. "I do not ask out of idle curiosity. I have need of the man. If you won't tell me where he is, I'll march through every racecourse in England until I find him. I want Martine and I want him now!"

The lad's head raised, his eyes widening in surprise at her furious tirade. Slowly a grin stretched across his face, and his eyes danced in appreciation.

"Sound jest like your da," Tim said.

"You owe the same loyalty to me that you paid to Sir George." Jena still spoke firmly, no answering smile on her lips.

"He willna want you to see him, miss."

"Not at first, perhaps." Now Jena's smile broke through and she grinned cheekily at the goggling boy. "Just give me time, Tim."

Catching his breath at the beauty revealed by the smile, Tim stood mesmerized for a moment. Then he caught the look of determination in her eyes and nodded his head in defeat.

"Worley Livery. East of town." Tim bit off each

word, his mouth tight with disapproval. "He's a room in back."

Once more Jena extended her hand. There was no hesitation this time as the boy eagerly clasped her fingers. "I'll send word when I need you," she said, her eyes steady on his face. She waited for the nod of acceptance before she released his hand. "Soon, Tim, soon."

Nanny muttered animadversions beneath her breath, but Jena ignored her, caught up in the whirl of thoughts in her head. From Tim's reluctance she suspected that Martine had fallen on hard times indeed. She must steel herself before she approached the man. Martine was a man of pride. One sign of pity and she would destroy him.

Wearily they trekked through Epsom, asking directions in the center of town. Worley Livery was a run-down, ramshackle affair, squatting on a barren patch of ground on the edge of town. Shingles were missing from the roof, and the building had a decided list to one side. Jena winced at the filth littering the yard. Swallowing a lump in her throat, she circled the building. The back was in even worse shape. A low, shedlike room jutted from the main barn. Determinedly, she made for the doorway. Raising a gloved hand, she knocked at the door. Silence met her, and clenching her jaw, she raised her fist and banged loudly on the scarred boards.

"G'way," came the slurred voice.

For a moment Jena weakened, closing her eyes in an agony of remembrance. Then biting the inside of her cheek, she hardened her heart. "Open this door at once!" she commanded.

Shuffling sounds met her ears and Jena squeezed Nanny's hand, drawing comfort from the heartening smile of the old woman. She waited nervously, then raised her hand a third time.

"S'open!" the snarling voice replied.

Jena dropped her hand, searching for the doorknob. Finding none, she pushed against the door and it wobbled open, banging loudly against the wall of the room. Light streamed through the doorway, spotlighting the disheveled old man, hunched over a battered oak table. Jena's heart sank at the disorder of the room. Worse than any pigsty, she muttered grimly. A rank odor assailed her, part unwashed body, part gin, and part accumulated dirt. Martine raised his head unsteadily, squinting at the shadowed figures silhouetted in the doorway.

"G'way," he repeated, letting his head drop to the cushion of his scrawny arm.

Jena's heart physically ached and she pressed a hand to her breast. She had seen the hopelessness written on the bewhiskered face of her friend and longed to hurl herself at him in comfort. Kindness, sympathy, compassion, all were destructive to a man's pride. Only cruelty could save him.

"Open those shutters, Nanny," Jena ordered, storming into the room. Her eyes blazed in her white face. A battered keg impeded her progress and she kicked out savagely, sending it tumbling across the beaten-earth floor with a satisfying clatter.

She ignored the groggy old man, waiting until Nanny pulled the shutters back to reveal the abject squalor of the room. Her eyes searched and found a broom, wedged into a corner beneath a pile of miscellaneous debris. She snatched it up, wielded it like a sword as she poked Martine in the shoulder with the wooden handle.

"Get up, you swill-belly!" she shouted. She had

97

no need to fabricate an anger, since it infuriated her that her friend had sunk to such degradation.

Slowly the shaggy salt-and-pepper-thatched head lifted. Rheumy eyes glared at her. Jena could almost see when the fog parted in his brain and a glimmer of recognition lit his eyes. Soul-wrenching anguish distorted his features, but she permitted no faltering of her own expression. Then his brow furrowed in confused puzzlement and his face sagged back into hopeless lines. Jena reversed the broom, sweeping it across the table to send the contents tumbling to the floor.

"How dare you ignore me, you worthless lout!" Jena slammed the broom onto the table directly in front of Martine. This time the man's jaw dropped as full awareness of her identity washed over him. "Don't just sit there gawking like some gape-seed. You're bloody well right it's me."

"Jena." There was a cry behind the whispered word, but Jena was in full swing now and she could not afford to soften.

"Lady Havenhurst, if you please," she snapped, her voice full of generations of aristocratic snobbery. She fumbled in her reticule and extended her purse to Nanny. "I want water, tea, and something to eat."

Without a backward glance, the old woman scuttled out the door. There was silence in her wake. Martine glared at Jena, but she refused to flinch at the flash of loathing she saw mirrored in his faded blue eyes. She knew he hated her for seeing him like this. In feigned indifference, she began to sweep the room, the violent strokes of the bristles the only visible sign of her agitation. Clouds of dust billowed up from the floor, but neither occupant acknowledged its presence. Martine remained immovable, his face a mask of animosity.

By the time that Nanny returned, some progress had been made. The floor of the room had been cleared and the refuse piled into one corner. Jena accepted the pot of steaming water from the urchin who had been pressed into service. Another scraggly youth extended a pot of tea and three chipped mugs. Nanny, her wrinkled face abeam, carried a small kettle of stew, complete with a wooden spoon and a loaf of bread in the crook of her arm. Triumphantly she plunked the food on the table and shooed the children out the door.

Jena dipped a rag into the water, meticulously wiping her face and her hands, ignoring the snort of scorn from the old man. She wiped the table and the bench beside it, then tossed the cloth across to the old man, her eyebrow lifted in challenge. His lip curled in a snarl, but beneath her intimidating gaze he struggled out of his chair. Jena let no hint of compassion tinge her expression.

Martine balanced on his massive arms, his one good leg unsteady on the floor. The trouser leg covering his stump flagged back and forth, brushing the chair with each movement. He hobbled to the pot, dipping the cloth into the water. He winced at the heat but plunged his hand in as if the pain could erase the other emotions beating in his brain. Once started, he vigorously scrubbed his face and neck, rubbing the skin red in his frenzy. Finally he threw the rag in the corner and hobbled back to his chair. Without a word, Jena shoved the kettle of stew in front of him. The wooden spoon followed, clattering against the oak tabletop.

"Tea, Nanny?" Jena asked. Her voice held only polite social interest, and with unconscious grace, she spread her skirts and seated herself at the table.

"Perhaps later, child," Nanny answered, smiling

warmly at the girl. "For the moment the thought of a nap is uppermost in my mind. It has been a long day and I find at my age a need to rest."

Nanny, winking conspiratorially over Martine's bent head, crossed the room to the cot against the wall. Jena watched in amusement as the old woman shook out the worn horse blanket covering the bed. Then, wrapping the colorful wool around her body, she sank gratefully onto the lumpy mattress.

Jena's hands were steady as she filled two mugs, pushing one across to the silently eating Martine. She picked up the bread, tearing off the heel. Her slim fingers made short work of the loaf, ripping it into edible sections. Finished, she raised the mug to her lips, sighing at the strong brew that filled her mouth. The coarse bread was fresh, and she closed her eyes and sniffed the crust, inhaling the warm, yeasty scent. When she opened her eyes, Martine was watching her, his face soft with remembrance.

"I need you, Martine," Jena said, for the first time letting emotion push the anger aside.

The old man's eyes went blank, shutting her out, and she cursed, fearing she had lost him. She waited in an agony of suspense, forcing herself to sip casually at her tea.

"Martine is dead," the old man whispered bitterly. "No one needs a one-legged man."

"Ask for no pity, man, and I'll give you none." Jena's words were cruel and she met the blaze of hatred without blinking. "I want to start up the stud again."

Martine's eyes momentarily widened with interest, then glazed over and stared down lifelessly at the stew. Carefully he lifted his spoon, shoveling the food into his mouth in a steady rhythm. Jena waited until he had finished and had wiped the last bit of gravy with a crust of bread.

"I'm in trouble, Martine. It's even worse than after Father died. I'm in a tight fix, but I have a plan," Jena said, her smile elfin with mischief. "It's a long shot and I need your help."

"You're wastin' your time," came the surly reply. "You can talk if you want, but it changes nothing."

Although the man remained hostile, Jena was encouraged that he would at least listen. Giving only limited details, she told him about the kidnapping and marriage to the viscount, the interview with the Duke of Wayfield, and then briefly outlined the circumstances and terms of the wager.

"I want to start up the stud. For all my father's improvidence, the reputation of Dunton Stud was above reproach. It can be again. I still own Dunton House. I've leased it, but the occupants keep only a few horses in the stables. It would be to their advantage if we reopened the stud. We could offer to care for their cattle without charge."

"We'd have to start small," Martine said, his voice hesitant as though he were thinking out loud. "How much money could you put into the stud?"

Jena dropped her eyes to the bread in her hands. Elation coursed through her body. The gypsy was hooked, she crowed. She kept her voice unemotional as she answered his question.

"I plan to use all of the lease money and half the allowance the viscount has given me for the start-up and maintenance of the stud." Jena waited while the gypsy stared into space, his mind clearly calculating.

"It would be far better if we had more," Martine said, rubbing his knuckles along his unshaven jawline. "When is the next rent payment?"

"In two days time," Jena said. She liked the conspiratorial smile that creased his face. Her heart felt lighter as she waited for him to continue.

"Let's assume for the moment that the stud is taken care of. How does this resolve anything? In the beginning it will bring no profit. It will just drain off your resources, and then you're bound to lose the wager. How do you expect to maintain your household on half your allowance?" Martine asked. "You've no servants, and you'll be able to hire nothing but the dregs on what is left."

"I'll hire only the needy. Those who are desperate for work. My thought is to offer food and board," Jena began. At Martine's snort of derision, she held up her hand imperiously. "Besides, each person who gives satisfaction will receive a share in the stud."

Martine's low whistle was an indication of his surprised approval. He eyed her steadily for a moment, his face reflecting a dawning respect.

"Equal shares?"

"I get forty percent. You get thirty. The final thirty will be split among the servants according to rank. Everyone works; everyone shares."

Silence filled the room. Martine stared at the girl, taking in the determined chin and the steady gaze of the gray eyes. She had grown into the beauty he had known she possessed. Her features were a composite of her parents', but her strength of character was all her own. The plan was risky at best, foolhardy at worst. Perhaps that was why it appealed to him.

"What do you want from me?"

Pleasure rippled through Jena at the look on his face. She felt confident now that he was in on the venture, and her heart filled to bursting.

"First and foremost, I want you to run the stud.

102

You'll have full authority. The money is yours to spend."

"No questions asked?" He eyed her blandly.

"I'll question you every step of the way, you black-hearted rogue," Jena said, chuckling at the wounded expression on Martine's face. "Knowing your silver tongue, I'll be lucky if I get a straight answer."

"What else do you need?" Martine asked, ignoring the amusement of the girl.

"I need servants. The best I can get. You know everyone around the racing circuit. Put out the word. My father was well-known, and there are many who would be glad to work for his daughter. I want those with experience in a gentleman's household who for some reason cannot find work. I want those who are in need, and I'll accept no slackers," Jena stated firmly.

"How much time have we got?"

"Three months. At the end of that time, if I have won the bet, the viscount should be interested in the stud as an investment. If I have lost the wager, we will have only the lease money to depend on, but at least we will have the hope of a future." Jena's face was serious as she stared across the table at her friend. "Is it workable, Martine?"

"I dunno, lass," the old man admitted, his seamed face showing honest concern. Then he lay a stubby finger beside his nose and gave her a broad wink. "Iffen I was a betting man, I'd plunk down the gold. It's fair risky, but I suspect with a few modifications we ought to be able to make a go of it."

Jena reached a shaking hand across the table. The old gypsy carefully picked it up, cupping it gently in the palm of one broad hand. With the other hand, he stroked the long, slim fingers of the girl, his mouth working with emotion. Slow tears trickled down Jena's cheek, but they were tears of joy for a friendship reborn.

Chapter Eight

Devereaux Havenhurst smiled smugly as he stared up at the stone facade of his town house. He was rested after his week's sojourn with his friends, but he suspected the new Lady Havenhurst had had a bad time of it. He could imagine the shambles that would greet him. Hopefully by now she had given up her quest for respectability and was prepared to be reasonable. Perhaps his dismissal of the servants had been less than sportsmanlike. He felt no compunction at the trick he had played, feeling that the conniving young woman had asked for that particular strategy. His friends did not call him the Gray Fox for naught.

He brushed a particle of lint from the sleeve of his tan superfine jacket, then fluffed the lace edging on his cravat. Max's valet had turned him out particularly fine for his interview with his wife. Dev suspected he would be subjected to tears and hysterics over the loss of the wager. He was prepared to be gracious, of course. He would wipe her tears and coax her to confide her troubles. At that point she would be more amenable to the annulment. And once Jena realized he was even planning to provide her with a generous settlement, she should be in a decidedly amiable frame of mind to entertain his newest proposal.

Now that the black-haired temptress was chastened, she should make an admirable mistress. Unless his memory was faulty, the girl was a prize indeed. He remembered the petal-soft skin that had begged to be touched, the pouting mouth ripe for his kisses. He groaned as he had all week when he imagined the lush figure writhing in his arms. Dev cleared his throat, passing a tongue over his suddenly dry lips. Enough of these puerile fantasies. It was time for action. He straightened his shoulders and, with the head of his cane, tilted his beaver hat to a more jaunty angle. Briskly he mounted the steps and raised his cane to alert the house of his return.

Before the cane could touch the wood, the door was pulled open from within. Dev's eyebrows raised in surprise as he stepped over the threshold.

"Welcome home, Lord Havenhurst."

The harsh whispered voice came from behind Dev and he whirled to face the speaker. At the sight that greeted his eyes, he inadvertently stepped back a pace. An enormous figure stood at attention in the marble hallway. The servant, dressed in bright yellow livery, had the body of a behemoth and the face of an unrepentant murderer. Hands the size of hams were extended for Dev's hat, gloves, and cane. Behind him the door closed, cutting off any hope of escape.

"I am your new butler, milord," the man said in a voice with the rasp of sandpaper. "The name is Lamb."

"Devil, you say!" Dev blurted out.

Immediately his eyes flew to the expressionless butler, but Dev could see no flash of hostility to signal an imminent attack. He was mesmerized by the eye-catching splendor of the man's livery, which gave a certain justification to the thought that Dev had somehow stepped back in time. The butler was wearing elaborate court dress that was popular sometime in the early seventeenth century. From the cut of the full-skirted coat and the matching pantaloons, the "court" was most probably Russian. And yellow, by Gad. Lamb looked like some great vicious canary.

Slightly flustered, Dev removed his gloves and hat. He reluctantly released the cane, only because he felt it was beneath him to tug it away from the iron grip of the butler. Impassively, Lamb snapped his fingers, and a footman, wearing the same ludicrous apparel, crossed from an alcove to take the items.

"Perhaps milord would care to wait in the drawing room while I inform her ladyship of your arrival," Lamb rasped out.

"Thank you, eh, Lamb." Dev felt out of his depth, unbalanced by the calm efficiency of the butler. As he followed the stiff-backed man, he noted that the house appeared much as he had left it. Except that all the furnishings fairly gleamed with cleanliness.

At Lamb's signal, two footmen leaped to attention and flung open the drawing room doors. Though impeccably dressed in the same fanciful livery, the men's faces held the unmistakable scars of some pitched battle one would prefer not to hear about. The butler bowed in the doorway, backing into the hall as the doors closed in unison. Dev remained staring at the doors, unsure if he had dreamt the entire episode.

"What May game is the wench up to?" Dev muttered under his breath.

He paced to the fireplace, clearly disgruntled. He had expected a household in chaos and a weeping bride, eager to admit defeat. Instead he was greeted by a gang of costumed brigands whom he suspected would be more eager to relieve him of his purse than his hat and gloves. He would have to be firm with his soon-to-be mistress and get to the bottom of this puzzle. Behind him the doors were flung open and Dev whirled to face the new Lady Havenhurst.

"Welcome home, Lord Havenhurst," she said, dropping into a graceful curtsy.

Dev had only seen Jena in a rumpled brown gown, hair pulled simply to the nape of her neck. He could not believe that the vision who approached him was the same woman. She wore a simple round dress of the softest peach tones, which brought a flush of color to her skin. Her glorious black hair was piled on top of her head in a Psyche knot, artful wispy curls brushing her shell-like ears. Unconsciously he moved forward, extending his hand to raise her to her feet.

Thick black lashes surrounded the wide gray eyes staring steadily up at him. Dev was caught by her glance, his senses expanding in the magic of her gaze. Then she blinked and he returned to earth.

"I'm delighted to see your allowance was not wasted," Dev sneered. He dropped her hand and stepped back to survey her. "You look exceptionally well, Lady Havenhurst."

"No need for such formality," Jena said, ignoring his sarcasm. "Please call me Jena."

She crossed to the couch, spreading her skirts carefully across the white satin cushions. The furious beat of her heart sounded loud to her ears and she hoped he was not aware of her agitation. She had forgotten what a handsome man the viscount was. During the week that he was away she had seen him in her mind as some monstrous, loathsome creature. His size was a dash intimidating, but his hawklike features and white hair were vastly appealing. She controlled her wandering thoughts and chastized herself for her inattention. Much depended on this interview.

"Won't you sit down, milord," Jena said, annoyed at the slightly breathless quality to her voice. "Since I'm sure after your travels you would welcome some sustenance, I have instructed Lamb to bring an early tea."

"Where in God's name did you get that man, Jena?" Dev asked. "He's obviously a murderer!"

"Softly, milord. You'll hurt his feelings."

"Feelings, my dear woman?" Dev whispered, casting a worried glance in the direction of the doors. "The only thing he'll ever feel is the hangman's rope."

"Really, milord, there's no need to carry on so. Lamb is an excellent butler," she defended. "Granted, he has a slightly daunting presence."

"Daunting! We'll be lucky if we're not all murdered in our beds. And what happened to his voice? Does he always whisper like that?"

"An unfortunate accident, milord," Jena admitted, busily pleating the skirt of her dress. "Apparently, a friend of his tried to cut his throat."

"Good Lord! It needed only that," Dev said, slapping his forehead with the palm of his hand.

As the doors were flung open, Dev jerked around as though fearing attack. Lamb entered the room, followed by two older women, bearing silver trays. Dev blinked in disbelief at the outlandish dirndls, frothy petticoats, and white, laced blouses reminiscent of waitresses in a beer hall. The dainty mobcaps added a piquant touch, emphasizing the raddled features of the old ladies. One of the biddies deposited the heavy silver tea tray in front of Jena, and the other set a large tray covered with sand-wiches and pastries beside it.

"Will there by anything else, your ladyship?" the butler grated.

"No, thank you, Lamb. This should do quite nicely." Jena smiled warmly up at the man.

Lamb snapped his fingers and the maids bobbed a curtsy and scurried from the room. As before, the butler backed from the room and the doors silently closed, cutting him off from sight.

"Does he always leave the room that way?" Dev asked curiously, having to tear his eyes away from the doorway.

"Yes, milord," Jena answered. She was glad her hand was steady as she poured a cup of tea. She raised it and Dev took it absently, his mind clearly still on the butler. "Please help yourself, milord. I believe Cook sent along some cucumber sandwiches as well as the sweets."

"Dare I ask what idiosyncracies Cook possesses?" Dev drawled. "A penchant for arsenic? Or is she content with the common rat poisons?"

"Truly, milord, she is nothing out of the way. She is a positive miracle worker with pastries, and her fish course would make Prinny weak with envy. You will find no fault with her sauces, and I promise you her pheasant presentation is something to behold. Of course, she is blind in one eye," Jena said, her eyes twinkling as Dev's hand hovered over the tray of food. "But before you ask how, I warn you the word 'gouged' might dampen your appetite."

"Good God!" Dev swore, snatching his hand back from the sandwiches.

At the horrified expression on Dev's face, Jena could contain her laughter no longer. She tried to stifle it behind a hastily raised napkin, but the more she attempted to gain control, the less successful she was. Her shoulders were shaking and her eyes watering before she gave in to the gales of laughter that rolled through her body. Dev drew himself up, greatly affronted, but this only added to Jena's amusement.

Dev was furious when the bold jade began to laugh. He glowered across the tea table wanting nothing more than to strangle her. Despite his anger, his hauteur dissolved in the face of such natural amusement. There was nothing coarse or vulgar about the girl's merriment. Even her laughter had a musical sound, he thought in bemusement. There was a freedom evident in her gaiety that he had not seen in his previous dealings with her. At their last interview, she had been suspicious and wary of his every movement. And behind that distrust he had seen a shadow of what he thought had been desperation.

Reseating himself, Dev raised his cup, sipping slowly while he examined the girl. There was a glow about her that had been totally missing the last time he saw her. It had nothing to do with her beauty. She had been then, and was now, an exquisitely beautiful woman. Yet there was a difference. As he examined her face he was conscious of a strength and assurance she had not originally exhibited. The image of a cornered animal rose in his mind, and Dev realized it was that picture of the girl he had carried with him during his week of hunting.

"My apologies, milord," Jena said, wiping the tears from her eyes. "I fear I have been exceedingly nervous about your return and I have behaved unforgivably."

"There is no apology needed, my dear," Dev said. Surprisingly, he meant it. He was no longer offended at her laughter at his expense. Perhaps he had deserved it. "If you can assure me that I will not rapidly meet my Maker, I would be happy to sample Cook's offerings."

Once Dev had eaten several examples of his new cook's culinary skills, he was ready to admit that he would keep her on were she blind in both eyes. Although they spoke mere pleasantries, there was not a stilted quality to the conversation. Dev discovered that Jena was apparently educated enough to hold her own in a discussion.

"One more pastry, milord?" Jena asked, pointing to a luscious cherry tart.

"At the rate I am going, at the end of three months, I will have gained six stone," Dev replied, shaking his head.

The mention of the wager cast a pall on the light atmosphere they had maintained. Dev was thoroughly irritated, since he discovered that he had been enjoying himself. He regretted the return of wariness in Jena's face. He frowned at her downcast eyes and her hands, which were once more pleating her skirt in neat folds.

"Stop that," Dev snapped.

Her eyebrows arched in surprise at his sudden outburst. But then even he was taken unawares by the flash of annoyance at Jena's withdrawal.

"Milord?" Jena asked.

"And don't call me milord," he ordered. He was discomfited by the triviality of his anger. "My name is Devereaux. Friends call me Dev."

"And which would you prefer?" Jena's voice was cool, showing only polite interest.

"Dev," came the muttered reply.

"Thank you, uh, Dev; I shall endeavor to remember that. Are there any other preferences that I should know about?"

For an instant he thought she was being coyly flirtatious, but one look at the innocent eyes raised to his disabused him of the idea. For some unknown reason a flush of color rose from his collar and he shifted uncomfortably in his chair.

"I hope you will find the staff satisfactory," Jena said, anxious to discover his reaction. "They are still learning some of their duties, but so far I have had little complaint with their services."

Grateful to have a topic on which to vent his rising anger, Dev rose to his feet, pacing across to the mantel. "Where did you unearth such a scurvy lot? I have not seen such an assemblage of viperous miens since I last visited Newgate Prison."

"You have only yourself to blame, Devereaux," Jena said, steel beneath the softly spoken words. "With the money you allotted, I was hard-pressed to convince anyone to work here. I'll admit that they appear a dash less than prepossessing." She ignored Dev's ungracious snort of derision. "But those that I have hired really need employment. It is my hope that their loyalty and enthusiasm will offset any flaws in their appearance. Besides, their impeccable livery lends a certain cachet to the household."

Again Dev thought he caught a hint of dry sarcasm in Jena's words, but her gray eyes were serene in the lovely face. "Ah, yes. The livery. Quite dashing, I must admit," Dev drawled. "Might I inquire what seamstress I have to thank for that creation? I'm quite convinced such originality must be prodigiously expensive."

"So delighted you like it," Jena said, trying to keep a straight face. "But never fear, milord, um, Dev, I would not be so profligate with my allowance. A lucky happenstance occurred that I felt fated to solve some of my financial difficulties."

113

"I find, my dear, I am fair breathless with anticipation."

Jena ignored the mockery in his voice. "Word came to me that one of the theatrical groups had run into financial embarrassment. *Les Trois Arts.* True to their name, they were devoted to the three arts: music, acting, and dance. I was unfamiliar with the troupe but understood their difficulties lay in the lavishness of their undertakings. You know the sort of thing," Jena said, waving a delicate hand airily. "Expensive costuming, too large a cast, and poor attendance."

"Tsk, tsk," Dev said, a mournful concern furrowing his brow. *"C'est bien dommage."*

"Exactly." Jena smiled with genuine amusement at her husband's teasing words. "I was told that their last performance quite took one's breath away. It was a farce by Stalworth entitled: *Die Mädchen und Die Herren von des König.* Rather a stirring drama with an enormous amount of singing and bloodletting. A tragic tale, I gather."

"Let me guess," Dev said. He acknowledged the mischievous twinkle in Jena's eye with an answering smile. " 'The Maiden and the King's Gentlemen' would I suspect be the proper translation. Hmm. I have it. Poor but virtuous young girl forced to work for her living in a dance hall near court. King falls madly in love with her, but his noblemen thwart his efforts to marry her. Alone and slightly less virtuous, she kills herself in an agony of despair."

Jena applauded spiritedly and Dev flourished his arm in a dramatic bow of appreciation. He joined in her laughter, delighted that he could so entertain her.

"Very inventive, Dev," Jena cheered. "You were

114

close enough; however, in the version I heard, the maiden was only poor."

"How scandalous! Can't imagine why their attendance was poor, since generally the public adores licentious entertainment."

Jena refused to rise to the bright gleam in his eyes. "Well, in any case, the troupe was disbanding. Nanny and I visited the theater and, after discovering the extent of their wardrobe, decided that it was the answer to our own problem of outfitting the servants."

"Most inventive, my dear," Dev said admiringly. "Can I hope that you only purchased the wardrobe from their last bravura performance?"

At Jena's pursed mouth and sadly shaking head, Dev gave a great shout of laughter. He could not recall when he had been so amused. Finally he was able to ask, "Would you care to enlighten me as to the other theatricals to which I may look forward?"

"I think not, sirrah," Jena said, feigning indignation at his teasing. "It will have to be a pleasure postponed."

"It must have been an enormous cast if you were able to outfit the entire staff," Dev remarked.

"We did have to make some substitutions for the kitchen helpers, but on the whole we contrived. Which reminds me, Dev. I was not sure whether you would wish me to engage a valet or you would prefer your own man."

The very stillness of the beauty warned Dev that trickery was afoot. He stared at her demurely bent head and an alarm rang along his nerves. Although he had been enjoying himself since his arrival, it was no intent of his to continue any longer in the marriage than was necessary. Jena had managed to circumvent the immediate forfeiture of the wager by a clever use of her moneys. It would not do to underestimate the scheming minx.

"According to the wager, I have given you full authority over my household, madam," Dev said agreeably. "You must provide adequately trained servants. Any valet you choose will have to keep me slap up to the mark. In the first stare of fashion, don't you know."

"Naturally, Lord Havenhurst," Jena said. She kept her tone bored, showing not an ounce of the nervousness she was feeling. "If you would be so kind as to ring."

Dev pulled the bell cord, then wandered back to the fireplace, consciously steeling himself for the opening of the doors. He was proud when only his pulse leaped as the doors were flung back.

"Lamb, would you send for Weatherby," Jena asked.

The doors closed and Dev hid a smile behind his hand. He could already picture Weatherby. Starchy and supercilious. Convinced he knew the latest trends. Probably worked for a cit with high expectations. Dev's eyes never left the carved doors, relishing the set-down he would give the man. He barely even cringed when the portals were flung open to reveal the valet.

"You be wantin' me, missus?" asked the chirping voice of the little man in the doorway.

So opposite was Weatherby to what Dev had expected that he wanted to roar with laughter. He bit the inside of his cheek in an effort to hold back his amusement. In her inexperience, Jena had hired a common sailor to valet him. On short banty legs, the man swaggered into the room. He stopped, planting his feet squarely on the carpet as though riding the quarterdeck of a bucking schooner. While the other servants had been meticulously turned

116

out, Weatherby's slapdash appearance was almost an art form. His coat was unbuttoned and his pantaloons rode low on his hips. Sparkling brown eyes peered out of a nest of wrinkles on his tanned face.

"Dev, this is Weatherby," Jena said.

"G'day, Cap'n." The man saluted jauntily, his leathery skin puckered in a cheerful smile.

"And a good day to you." Dev could not resist a grin of his own. "Have you been long in service?"

"Not so's you'd notice," Weatherby said, scratching some unknown spot beneath his jacket. "Spent most of me life at sea."

"I suspicioned as much," Dev said, his voice dry. "I hope we'll suit, but I must admit that I am rather particular about my turnouts."

"A bucko with your figger? Well, I should say so, Cap'n. And I'm prepared to do you up proud."

Dev shuddered, imagining what the little man had in mind. He felt slightly nonplussed that his win of the wager was being made so easy. He glanced at Jena, wanting to spare her feelings at the debacle. Her eyes were soft as she smiled encouragement to the stocky jack-tar. He wondered how she could ever have expected him to find the man acceptable. Well, there was nothing for it. A few more questions for the sake of form.

"A Londoner?" Dev asked.

"Aye, Cap'n. Born in the shadow of the docks."

More likely conceived in the shadow of the docks, Dev thought. "Your name is quite suitable for a gentleman's valet."

"Thankee, sir. Weatherby was me old mum's idea," he announced proudly. "Didn't rightly know who me father was. Used to say, 'Don't know whether be this one or whether be that one.' Ever since, I've been called Weatherby."

It took a moment before the pun penetrated Dev's

brain. When it did, his eyes began to tear and his mouth worked as though he were in pain. Turning, he clung to the mantelpiece, while behind him he heard Jena's quietly spoken words.

"That will be all for now, Weatherby."

"Aye, aye, missus."

At the sound of the closing door, Dev burst into laughter. He turned to Jena, who was chuckling behind the fingers covering her mouth. Their eyes touched and Dev was shocked at the pleasure he felt in the shared joke.

"Madam, my congratulations," he said, sweeping her a deep bow. He crossed the room, flopping down casually into the chair beside the sofa. "Weatherby is a jewel indeed."

"How could I have turned him away?" Jena asked. "I knew you would appreciate the drollery."

Strangely enough, it was true. She had known Dev for such a short time, and the majority of that had been full of fury, acrimony, and deceit. Yet intuitively Jena sensed that Dev had a wry sense of humor, an ability to find great amusement in the smallest detail. When she thought of it, she was shocked at the risk she had taken in hiring the unqualified sailor. Dev could have cried forfeit if he had chosen. Although she was suspicious and distrustful of his methods to win the wager, she had believed that he would not hold her to the letter of the law. Perhaps she wanted to believe there was some good in the viscount, her mind suggested. Jena fussed with the tea things and studied her husband.

She was surprised to note that his good humor had vanished, to be replaced by a face set in a brown study.

Beware of the clever little wench, Dev reminded himself. He could not believe that he had been so

118

bewitched by her jest over Weatherby that he had not immediately called for an end to the wager. It would be ungentlemanly to cry foul at this late date. He would just have to be more on his mettle. After all, he had no intention of remaining married to the minx. He did not want to be married.

He enjoyed his life, his freedom. Certainly, since his arrival, he had been delightfully entertained by the lovely baggage, but after all, this was not a real marriage. He might enjoy Jena's company for an hour or two, but he would eventually become bored, and then, God forbid, he would become dull company.

He had to admit his new bride was a joy to behold. Wispy black tendrils had slipped from her topknot and clung to the side of her neck. Her features had the purity of a cameo, he thought. He liked the silky material of her dress and the way it clung to her figure. When she first entered the room, he had been conscious of the long legs beneath her skirt. He wondered if she could ride. He liked the feel of tight muscles beneath satiny skin.

Dev looked up, and Jena was watching him. His eyes held hers and he watched with satisfaction as the awareness of him came into the pools of gray. Perspiration broke out on his upper lip. His eyes dropped to her mouth, which was slightly parted. Her tongue flicked out, moistening the full bottom lip.

"I'm going to my club," Dev announced, jumping to his feet. "Do not expect me for dinner."

Without a backward glance, Dev strode to the doors. He flung the panels open, nearly crushing the startled footmen. Silently the doors closed behind him.

Jena remained seated, her hands firmly gripped together. She was not surprised at his abrupt de-

119

parture. She was grateful. At least she ought to be, she muttered. She had seen the heated look in his eye and was not too innocent to misunderstand the meaning. Desire was clear for her to read. Her relief was in the fact that he had not been aware of her response. She could still feel the blood pounding in her temples. What had come over her?

Since she had met Lord Devereaux Havenhurst, she had been in danger. She had been able to protect herself so far because she had been angry and desperate to win the wager. At risk were her name, her honor, and her financial security. And unless she was very careful, she would be risking far more. She would be risking her heart.

Chapter Nine

Jena's satin slippers were silent on the hall runner as she followed the sound of the piano to the music room. She stood in the doorway amazed at the proficiency of her husband. At the end of a particularly lovely piece, Dev looked up and Jena flushed guiltily as if caught spying. Since his return two days earlier, she had studiously avoided his company.

"You needn't look so stricken. I am not an ogre!" Dev snapped, annoyed at the look of fear on the girl's face. Then hearing the harshness of his voice, he grinned suddenly. "At least not all the time."

"I'm sorry for interrupting," Jena apologized. "I couldn't help myself. You play beautifully."

"No point in standing in the hall." Dev waved her negligently into the room. "I play for my own amusement, but if you enjoy it, you are welcome to join me."

"Would my presence be intrusive?" Jena asked.

"In truth, madam, when I play I lose contact with the world," Dev answered, brushing his long fingers through his hair as though embarrassed by the admission.

Watching Dev gave Jena a new awareness of her husband. He had spoken truly when he said she would not be intruding. For the most part he ig-

121

nored her, his eyes closed as his strong hands glided across the keys. Her eyes followed the movements of his hands as he pounded out the heavier Beethoven concertos or coaxed sweet sentiment from a Mozart sonata. His relaxed features reflected the emotion of each piece, and Jena read the complexity of his character in the range of his expressions.

Day after day she enjoyed the after-breakfast musicales, sitting quietly while the music rolled over her. Usually it was a relaxing hour, but one morning Jena found the music less than soothing. She was in a restless mood, tired of reading and bored with her housekeeping duties. She was feeling curiously depressed and decided a brisk walk in the park would blow away the cobwebs in her head.

"I say, Jena, are you feeling quite the thing?"

Dev's question broke into Jena's thoughts and she wondered for a moment if he was able to read her mind. She suspected he'd spoken to her earlier, but she had been so busy with her own thoughts, she had failed to notice.

"I'm sorry, Dev, I was wool-gathering," she apologized. "Thank you for your concern."

"You look a little pale. Are you getting out at all?"

"Occasionally," Jena answered cautiously. "Mostly shopping. Sometimes a walk. I am conducting myself discreetly since we are not officially at home to society."

"It was not my intent to keep you a prisoner." Dev shifted uncomfortably on the piano bench. "I was planning to attend an art gallery early tomorrow morning, and if you had nothing planned, you might consider coming along. The crowds are thin at that hour, so you needn't feel rushed. 'Course, you might consider that bland fare for an outing."

"I should like it very much," she answered softly.

In the days that followed, Jena found herself accepting Dev's offhand invitations with some misgivings. She was not convinced that his solicitude for her health did not hide some more nefarious motive. The outings ranged from pretentious art gallerys to simple tea shops. Occasionally he took her up in his curricle, tooling purposefully through the city streets until they reached the more countrified roads at the edge of town. She especially enjoyed the drives, finding Dev an amusing companion whether engaged in a light banter or a more serious discussion.

She noticed that the outings were all conducted in the early part of the day, when the chances of meeting any of the *ton* were negligible. Their relationship had become so relaxed that one morning Jena twitted him for being ashamed of being seen with her.

"Quite the contrary, my dear," he drawled.

Dev scrutinized the steady gait of his grays, shifting the reins into one hand before he turned to face her. Tousled by the wind, his white hair caught the sunlight, a halo above his saturnine features. He cocked his head, his eyes running coolly over her, and she stared straight ahead, hating the flush of color that rose to her cheeks under his scrutiny. She was sorry she had brought up the subject, yet she found herself holding her breath for his answer.

"You would not be an embarrassment in any company, Jena." Dev's voice held a note of quiet judgment, but beneath his words there was an unaccustomed warmth. "It should come as no surprise to you that I find you a most beautiful woman."

"Please," Jena said, writhing under his examination. "My tongue is too quick to make a joke. I was not begging for a compliment."

"I know you weren't. That's why I proffer it freely."

At the sincerity in Dev's tone, Jena's eyes flashed to his face. There was a fluttering in her midsection, which she had noticed occurred with great regularity when she stared into his clear blue eyes.

"Thank you for taking me for a drive today," Jena answered as steadily as she could. She was anxious to change the subject. "I'm country-raised and have never gotten used to the closed-in feeling of London air."

Dev's eyes crinkled at the corners as though he was aware of her strategy. Then in the lightning change of mood that Jena was becoming used to, his mouth thinned as his eyes once more swept her fashionable outfit. "I can see that your allowance is being put to good use. Very fetching bonnet, my dear. I have noticed that all your gowns have a certain understated elegance that comes from giving custom to a first-class modiste."

Now it was Jena's turn to find amusement in his words. Her eyes sparkled beneath the straw brim and her mouth was drawn into a wide smile, lips matching the dusky rose bow that nestled against her cheek.

"I'm delighted that you approve my wardrobe. After all, I must dress as befits your exalted rank in society," Jena said. Her tone was demure with only a hint of sarcasm. "I am well pleased with my seamstress, milord."

Inwardly Jena chuckled when Dev harumphed and returned his attention to the horses. Her wardrobe was a source of great amusement to her. She had realized immediately that to visit a well-known modiste would be to court financial disaster. One ball gown, let alone the amount of apparel she needed to be outfitted correctly, would cost the earth. After giving it considerable thought she had approached the fearsome Lamb with her requirements. Two days later Becky Homenecky was shown into the drawing room.

Jena had eyed the slender, soberly dressed young woman, guessing her age at twenty. She was struck immediately by the quiet elegance of the girl's dress, which at first glance was nothing remarkable until one took the time to analyze it. The cut, line, and detailing of the gown showed a flare for originality that pleased Jena. The dress did not conform strictly to the current fashion but instead used the assets of the girl's figure to rise above the norm.

In short order Jena had the girl's history. Becky had just opened a shop catering primarily to cits and others interested in clothes in the first stare of fashion. There was a strength of will evident in the girl that spoke of a confidence in her talents and a hunger for advancement. After much thought, Jena made her proposal.

Becky would provide Jena with a full wardrobe. The girl could indulge her originality as long as each item had taste and elegance. For her part, Jena would pay for the materials and trimmings. And of course, once she made her bow to society, she would laud Becky's skill to her friends.

Jena approved the guarded calculation in Becky's face. Her eyes carefully neutral, the girl studied the features and figure of her would-be patroness, missing nothing. After several minutes of unblinking regard, Becky nodded, her mouth widening into a conspiratorial grin. They set about immediately planning her wardrobe. As she listened to Becky's ideas for colors, styles, and materials, Jena was

125

convinced that she had made the right choice. Each item delivered confirmed her trust in the youthful seamstress.

Three weeks after their marriage, Jena sat in the drawing room frowning over her needlework. As she and Dev waited for tea, she wondered if they had reached the end to the uneasy truce they had established. She kept her head bent over her sewing, only occasionally peeking through her lowered lashes at the glowering figure in the chair beside the fireplace. Although he had been cheerful enough when he entered, after perusing the mail, Dev had fallen into a brooding silence. His eyebrows were bunched in concentration and his mouth drawn into a grim line. From time to time he tapped the thick envelope in his lap with the fingertips of one hand.

The drawing room doors were flung open with the usual unpredictable flurry, and Dev, caught off guard, leaped from his chair, scattering the mail on the carpet in a shower of envelopes. He leaned over to retrieve the letters, glaring malevolently at the stone-faced butler.

"Your tea, milady," Lamb rasped without glancing in Dev's direction.

Jena's eyes glittered wickedly as she caught the dark shadow of annoyance on Dev's face. She knew that her husband was thoroughly flustered by the butler, but it had become a point of honor for him never to admit the fact. Dev hated the unexpected bursting open of the drawing room doors but could not bring himself to mention it. His behavior amused Jena. When she rang the bell for tea, Dev invariably tensed, watching the clock and trying to guess when the doors would spring open. As though Lamb sensed the game, Jena noticed that the butler never arrived at the same time two days running.

"Will there be anything else, milord?"

Dev's features were carefully bland as he reseated himself in his chair. Calmly he looked up at the butler, shaking his head in negation. Only after the man backed out of the room and the doors clicked shut did he give vent to his temper, swearing under his breath.

"Are you quite positive, Jena, that Lamb is not wanted by Bow Street?" Dev snarled through gritted teeth. "An ax murder possibly or, at the very least, the strangulation of his mother?"

"Really, Devereaux," Jena chuckled. "Lamb is a wonderful butler."

"Umm," he said, unconvinced.

In truth she was amazed at how well all of the servants had done. Martine had spread the word, and Jena had been overwhelmed at the number who had applied. One and all they claimed friendship with Sir George Christie. Among the lower classes in the horse world, her father had been well respected and, when he was flush, extremely generous to those down on their luck. The people who arrived on her doorstep were an unprepossessing lot and very definitely in need of the work. The ones she chose all had experience in service but, for one reason or another, were unemployable. Some were too old. Others were scarred or infirm. Most had been let go without a reference, thus preventing them from applying for another respectable position. She assumed that some had fallen afoul of the law, and she suspected that several of the maids had been victims of lecherous employers.

Jena had explained that their past history meant nothing to her. First-class service and unfailing honesty were her only criteria. She would give them a chance to prove themselves for food, board, and a share in the stud farm. She promised that if they performed their duties well, she would give them an excellent reference in the event they decided to leave. The dazed look of pleasure on each of the faces convinced Jena that she had found a loyal staff. Without exception the servants had blended eagerly into a united work force.

Jena sipped her tea, conscious of Dev's brooding silence. Setting her cup down with a sharp click, she once more picked up her needlework. "Is something the matter, Dev?" she asked.

"Beg pardon?"

"You have been scowling at me for a full ten minutes. Have I done something to displease you?"

"Of course not, Jena," Dev said. "As always, you are a delight to the eye. Another lovely gown, I see. Very becoming, like all the others."

"I appreciate your approval. Would you care for more tea? It's an excellent restorative."

"Don't fuss at me, madam," Dev snapped. "Have I no right to ill humor? I cannot be unfailingly cheerful, like Lamb."

Jena's eyebrows raised, but she refused to dignify his sarcasm with a reply. She resumed her sewing, occupying her hands while her mind debated the source of his anger.

Unrepentant, Dev glared at the modestly bent head of black curls. He was annoyed that his outburst had ruined the harmony of their afternoon. She should have expected the set-down once she realized he was out of sorts. Perhaps she hadn't noticed. That thought further nettled him and, to pay her back for her inattention, he resolved to spend the rest of the evening at his club.

Damn and blast his interfering grandfather! It was the duke's letter that had sent him into such

a fit of the sullens. The Duke of Wayfield had com-
missioned an investigation of Jena; the completed
report lay unopened in Dev's lap. His hands gripped
the edges of the heavy envelope while a bleakness
entered his soul.

The duke's cover letter had given no indication
of the contents of the report. It informed him
bluntly that he had enclosed an entire history of
the girl Dev had married. It covered her family
background, her childhood, and her time spent in
London. All in all a comprehensive and detailed
document.

Dev's fingers stroked the envelope, the urge to
rip open the flap nearly overwhelming. If he read
the report, he would know without question who
she was. Lady Jena Christie, daughter of Sir George
Christie, or Jena Christie, actress? A lady or a
lightskirt? Or both, an insidious voice whispered in
his ear.

Even if the report proved that she was a gentlewoman, it would not convince Dev that she was a
woman of virtue. No woman of sensibility would
ever consider working in a theater. Even in desperate circumstances there were more respectable avenues of employment. A governess, companion, or
even shop assistant. A woman as refined and educated as Jena would have little difficulty finding a
suitable position. Only a woman of easy virtue who
hoped to better her station in life would work in a
theater.

Rich and titled men haunted the opera and theater specifically to discover a fresh face and figure
to pique their jaded palates. Dev ground his teeth
picturing Jena entertaining some aged peer. His
dry hands would rasp against her velvet skin as he
fastened a ruby necklace around her white throat.

Or worst yet, some burly cit, with no finesse, would bruise her arms in an awkward embrace.

Dev's eyes were haunted as he stared across at Jena's graceful form on the sofa. Did he want to know what hands had touched that skin or what arms had held that soft body? In one quick motion, Dev crossed the room and threw the report into the fire. He picked up the brass-handled poker and stabbed the envelope, watching in satisfaction as the flames licked up, consuming the whole. Replacing the poker, he turned to find Jena's curious eyes upon him.

"Only some useless papers," Dev said, his voice colorless. "Nothing that matters."

Curiously enough, it really didn't matter anymore, Dev thought as he stared down into the fire. He really didn't care who Jena was. He was content with her company for the moment and he would not permit his grandfather's interference to disconcert him.

Even if Jena could prove her good name, that question had been superseded by the wager. No matter who she was, if she won, he had agreed to accept the marriage. He must keep his mind on his priorities. He did not want to be married. That was the thing to remember. He must keep his head and do everything possible to win the wager. Once she agreed to the annulment, he could consider her background, but even then he suspected it would make no real difference. Whether she was spawned by a gin-swilling bawd or a perfumed lady, Dev intended to make Jena his mistress.

Chapter Ten

The three men huddled in funereal silence at one end of the table in the private dining room. From time to time they cast furtive glances at the dejected figure at the opposite end. Devereaux Havenhurst slumped on his spine against the carved back of his chair. His eyes were distant under lowered eyebrows, and from time to time he sipped unconsciously from the crystal goblet he held cradled against his chest.

"The Gray Fox has become dull company, gentlemen," Reggie mourned.

"Pass the bread, cuz," Dickon said, his eyes intent on his trencher of meat.

"Have you no thought for our friend, you insufferable churl? Stuffing your face in Devereaux's time of need," Reggie said, his whispered tone deeply censorious. However, when the enormous figure snarled at him, Reggie speedily reached for the bread, thrusting the basket beneath Dickon's nose.

"Think better on a full stomach." Dickon's beefy hand snaked out and he snatched a thick slice of bread. His face was intent as he methodically sopped up the drippings.

"What are we going to do, Max?" Reggie asked,

casting a concerned glance at the fastidious dandy across the table.

"Damn me if I know." Max smoothed the sleeve of his cerulean blue jacket, fluffing the lace at his cuff. He examined the fall of his cravat and made a minor correction to one of the folds before he cast a pensive look toward the end of the table. "Clearly our friend is unhappy."

Reggie ran a hand through his already disarranged blond curls. "He may be unhappy, Max, but what about us? Quite frankly, I'm exhausted. For the last month we have set a pace that would tire the most experienced campaigner. We have ridden to Richmond for a cockfight, to Bath for a mill, and three times to Newmarket for the races."

"Richmond had the best food," Dickon mumbled around a wad of bread.

Reggie ignored his cousin's interruption and continued his peroration of complaints. "We have hunted partridge the length and breadth of England and fished for trout until my valet turns bilious at the sight of my creel. We have seen every play, opera, and raree-show in London. We have gamed from White's to the meanest gambling hell. And to cap it off, we even put in an appearance at Almack's."

"Sally Jersey has not forgiven me for the punch incident on our last visit," Dickon interjected gloomily.

"Admittedly, gentlemen, life has been hectic of late, but it will pass," Max said. "Each day Dev's face gets longer and longer. He is coming to the realization that a constant round of entertainments will not resolve his problems."

"What's to do then?" Reggie asked.

"We wait," Max announced. "If my guess is correct, our friend will soon discover what ails him."

132

Although both Dickon and Reggie badgered the dandy, Max was adamant in his silence. He suspected he knew what drove Dev to the frenzy of activity. It had taken him a while to tumble to the truth. When they returned from the week at the shooting box, it seemed to Max that they were engaged every night. On closer examination, he discovered that they were only together every other night. Dev never mentioned what he did on his free nights, but it was curious.

The clincher came when Max realized that all the round of entertainments had been remarkably devoid of female companionship. Sports events, gaming, and carousing. All enjoyable male pursuits. At the plays, they had strolled in the pit. At the opera, they had occupied a box in chaste splendor. Even at Almack's, Dev stalwartly pressed them to do the pretty while he had stood glowering on the sidelines. One wondered how long they would be subjected to such a monklike existence. It amused Max that his longtime friend should be so little aware that he was suffering the pangs of love.

During the week after the midnight wedding, Dev had railed against the conniving wench who had lied to his grandfather in order to force him to accept the marriage. Although he still lamented the sly cleverness of the chit, Max noticed that his eyes did not flash with the same fire as originally. Instead there was a bewilderment to Dev's gaze, part confusion, part injury, and part self-doubt. It was apparent to Max that his friend was in a quandary.

Of special note was that, despite the fact Dev condemned the girl in their presence, he had done everything possible to protect her reputation. He had sworn the three friends to secrecy concerning the circumstances of the wedding and the wager. When they encountered anyone in society, Dev played the

133

part of the fortunate bridegroom, turning away most questions with a fatuous grin. Not by look or word did he indicate that there was anything unusual about their relationship. To the outside world Devereaux Havenhurst was a contented husband.

Max shook himself from his thoughts, rejoining the quiet talk of horses, women, and the latest scandals. So involved in their conversation were the three men that they were jolted by the pounding of Dev's fist on the table.

"Enough!" Dev shouted, glowering at the three men. His face broke into a smile at the startled expressions on his friends' faces. "I have become a dull dog indeed to so thoroughly ignore my companions of the evening."

"Have we offended?" Max drawled, one eyebrow cocked in question. His mouth was pursed in amusement and he fussed busily with the lay of watch fobs across his peacock-blue brocaded waistcoat.

"Offend? Never say, old man," Dev reproved. His eyes crinkled with good humor. "You have been boon companions this last month. You have followed without complaint on the merry chase I've led. What more could a friend ask?"

"Don't care what you say, Dev," Dickon said. "Not going one more place tonight. That squeeze at Lord Faversham's was a bust. The man's a pinchpenny when it comes to the buffet."

"Poor Dickon. It has been a lean week for you," Dev admitted. "I promise you will not need to worry. Tonight we shall make an early evening of it. I have been sadly blue-deviled, but I have sulked enough, and now it is time for action."

"Not another cockfight," Reggie groaned.

"Stubble it, lad," Dev said. "Quiet action is needed."

"To what benevolent god do we owe our eternal gratitude?" Max asked dryly.

"I had a letter from my grandfather."

There was a chorus of moans from the men, and Dev grinned as he raised his glass in silent agreement.

"If the duke is coming to town, I shall remove to the country," Reggie announced.

"No need for such drastic measures, old top," Dev said. "Grandfather threatened a return to town only in the eventuality that I ignored his latest missive."

"Not the first, I gather." Max searched Dev's shuttered expression, his own speculative. "What particular piece of advice have you been ignoring?"

Dev's eyes flashed in Max's direction. He did not like the calculated expression on his friend's face. The man was too perceptive, by half. And it was none of Dev's intent to permit anyone to grasp the real problem at hand.

"The Duke of Wayfield has commanded that I introduce my wife to society."

"I say, old bean, what a facer." Reggie grasped the decanter and hastily filled his glass. The frantic round of entertainments had permitted all of them to pretend that nothing had changed in their lives. Dev had explained the wager, and his friends had accepted the conditions without caviling. Beyond a bare statement of the situation, he had been less than forthcoming. Now the situation was changing, and Reggie did not like it. If Dev succumbed to the duke's edict, he would all but admit his married status.

Max placed his elbows on the table and leaned forward intently. He was unsurprised at the wariness in Dev's bearing. "The duke has mentioned this before?"

"Only in passing," Dev said, waving his hand airily. "I was hoping I could win the wager without resorting to such drastic measures. However, the clever wench has been able to survive quite well on the limited funds I have put at her disposal. The food at our table cannot be faulted. Nothing lavish, mind, but each dish a treat for the tongue. The servants, although the most scurvy lot, meet my every need for service. At times, I swear Lamb is a mind reader. Knows to a certainty whether I will require the carriage, curricle, or a horse."

Max smiled at the glum tone of the viscount's voice. It would have been more appropriate if he had been spewing a litany of complaints.

"Devil take it, Dev. Has even Weatherby turned into the perfect valet?" Reggie asked.

Dev pulled his earlobe, an abashed grimace lighting his face. "I fear perfect might be too strong a word," he admitted. "The man's taste in fashion is execrable. He is either color-blind or totally insensitive to my consequence. He prefers the gaudier apparel and would be in high alt if I would consider the extremes of the Macaroni."

"You look all the crack," Dickon said, his forehead furrowed as he examined the impeccable cut of Dev's black evening clothes and blindingly white linen. "Weatherby must be up to the mark."

"Hah!" Dev snorted. "Every morning the man thrusts a mug of tea under my nose and chirps, 'Well, Cap'n, what'll it be t'day?' I stagger out of bed and grope through my wardrobe and choose a suitable outfit for the day's activity. The wily old salt depends on the fact that I pride myself on my appearance. Despite his own slovenly appearance, he does keep everything shipshape, as he would say. But the little niceties that one expects from one's valet are beyond the man. He shaved me once, and the bloodletting was worse than any bearbaiting. Now, I ask you, gentlemen, is this any way to go on?"

Dickon guffawed and was joined by Reggie and Max. Even Dev's eyes twinkled with laughter, although his mouth was still set in disapproving lines.

"Why don't you fire the dolt?" Reggie asked curiously.

"I can't," groaned Dev. He leaned his elbows on the table and covered his face with his hands. Behind the protective shield, he spoke through his fingers. "He amuses me," came the muffled admission.

A combination of hoots and whistles sounded around the table. In embarrassment, Dev pushed his fingers through his white hair, his face a picture of chagrin.

"You're right. I'm a gudgeon. But, gentlemen, one look at that beaming monkey face and I turn hen-hearted. The man is unreservedly devoted to my every whim. Unfailingly cheerful. Unconditionally eager."

"And undeniably incompetent," Reggie finished waggishly.

"It seems to me, Dev," Max said, stroking his chin in puzzlement, "that the man's blatant ignorance is grounds for a forfeiture. According to the rules of the wager, your wife must provide adequate staff as befits your social consequence."

"Hear! Hear!" Dickon applauded loudly.

"I thought I explained this before," Dev said, drawing himself up in offended dignity. "I was bedazzled by the designing witch. Since I didn't cry foul immediately, it would be poor-spirited of me indeed to go whining to the woman due to a slight discomfort. Remember, Max, a viscount is first of all a gentleman."

"I stand in awe of your perception, old boy," Max drawled. "Then what say you now to the wager? Do you still plan to win?"

"Of course, you danderpate!" Dev shouted, glaring at the smirking man. "For your information, I have already decided to agree to my grandfather's commands. I shall host a party and put paid to the pretentions of my wife. Although I suspect that the whole evening will be a humiliating disaster, I will bear the brunt of the gossip-mongers' opprobrium."

"Excellent," Reggie said. "It'll prove once and for all that the bold piece slumguzzled you. Your scheming actress will see she is no match for the high-toned tabbies of society. She will find running a household is simple compared to organizing a first-rate *ton* entertainment."

"Good show, old man," Dickon said encouragingly. "We'll stand beside you. Shoulder to shoulder, that sort of thing."

"Could almost feel sorry for the lady," Max mused. "Society will make short work of her imposture."

"I appreciate your support, my friends," Dev said, ignoring Max's words. He pushed himself to his feet, staring somberly around the table. "Shall we say three weeks from tonight? After all, as a gentleman, I should offer my wife a sporting chance. For now, I am off. But never fear. I shall keep you apprised of developments."

It was still early enough for Dev to walk home, and he sauntered along the streets trying to extract some enthusiasm from his latest decision. His friends were right. He had dragged his feet too long over this matter. He needed to end the wager and get on with his life. Yet the prospect sent him deeper into the glooms. He didn't know why he should feel so dejected. It had been his intention all along to end the sham marriage. He should be looking forward to the denouement.

In a moment of honesty, Dev admitted that he liked the relationship that he had established with Jena. It was the awareness of this that had driven him to such a round of frenzied activity. Each hour he spent with her sent him fleeing in terror from an acceptance of the place she had carved out in his life.

At first he had been unaware of his dilemma. If he spent an evening with Jena, the next day he was filled with a restlessness to be with his friends. He had sought amusements away from his town house, yet had discovered the entertainments were sadly flat. More and more he looked forward to the quiet evenings at home. He had chided himself for acting like an aged fogy, worn out by social commitments. Soon he realized Jena was the magnet.

He had condemned marriage for making dullards of his friends. Now he understood that with the proper companion, one need never be bored. Jena continued to amuse him with her inventiveness. She was a delight to the eye. She was surprisingly well educated, with a mind curious and challenging. He thoroughly enjoyed their conversations, which ranged from a discussion of the Corn Laws to a hot debate over the formation of the land masses. She could be lightly teasing, coyly flirtatious, or devastatingly sarcastic. He was amazed at the complexity of her personality.

Approaching his doorway, Dev was unsurprised when, before he could knock, the door opened to admit him. Lamb, menacing as ever, accepted his garments.

"Good evening, milord," the butler rasped. "We did not expect you so early. Unfortunately, her ladyship has retired for the evening."

"It's of no consequence," Dev said, turning to the stairs. "I think I will follow her sterling example."

"Brandy, milord?"

"I'd appreciate it," he called over his shoulder.

When Dev opened the door of his room, Weatherby stumbled to his feet. He had been dozing before the fire, a mug of stout close at hand. He rubbed the sleep from his eyes while he tried to gauge the temperament of the viscount.

"Ev'ning, Cap'n," Weatherby said. He covered his yawning mouth with a hastily raised hand, then winked at the viscount's grin. "Mite early for you to be rollin' in, sir."

Dev shed his coat, handing it to the man, who scurried to help him undress. "I must be getting old, Weatherby," he said.

"Not you, Cap'n," his valet scoffed. "Prime o' your life. Perhaps you've been burnin' too many candles. Look a dash peaky."

Dev shrugged on his dressing gown and sank gratefully into the easy chair so recently occupied by the old sailor. A far cry from a night at sea, Dev thought, wondering if Weatherby missed his old life. The valet bustled around, putting Dev's clothes away. Finished, he saluted a good night as the butler entered with the brandy. Lamb rolled his eyes at the abandoned mug of stout, gingerly accepting it from Dev's outstretched hand. The stern-faced butler paused at the door, turning a jaundiced eye on the viscount.

"Her ladyship asked me to remind you that tomorrow is Wednesday. The servants' day off," Lamb announced.

The harsh whisper grated on Dev's already strained nerves. "Damn and blast!" He had been looking forward to a whole day with Jena.

"I could have Cook prepare you a cold collation for the evening," the butler suggested.

"Never mind, Lamb. I'll go to my club," Dev said in resignation.

"Will there be anything else, milord?"

Dev waved the man out of the room, muttering curses under his breath as he poured out the brandy. He should have been more authoritative when he explained to Jena that in a respectable household all the servants were never given the afternoon off on the same day. She had said she was sorry, that it had just seemed the simplest method. Why hadn't he explained that it would be inconvenient for him? Why had he let her have her way?

He was in love with Jena, that was the reason. Dev filled his mouth with the biting liquor, rolling it languorously over his tongue. He stretched his feet out and wriggled his toes to ease some of his tension. How could he, with all his experience, have fallen under the spell of an actress?

A vision of wide gray eyes and a billowing cloud of black hair formed in his mind. He loved to watch Jena when she was unconscious of his stare. Then his eyes could roam over her at will, touching where his hands could not. He admitted that the physical desire for her was an almost constant agony. However, he realized he would never be content with mere lovemaking. He wanted all of her. He wanted her mind and her heart, as well as her body. He could never make her his mistress. He would not so demean the lady.

Dev smiled when he remembered that the reason he had demanded release from the marriage was that she was not a lady. In his life, the social levels were clearly defined. Lady was reserved for a woman born with the proper parentage. He had come a long way in the realization that Jena might

141

not have been born a lady, but in her nature she was one. She possessed all of the qualities engendered in the title. She was gracious, kind, and virtuous. She had a fineness of character and a beauty of soul that many of the titled gentlewomen could not claim. And Dev wanted Jena for his lady.

Would Jena agree to starting the marriage over? She had been adamant that she must have the protection of his name, but that was a far cry from the relationship Dev envisioned. Could she ever come to love him? Admittedly, she had every right to hate him, and perhaps in the beginning she had. Since they had been seeing more of each other, he noticed that she had softened toward him. She had a welcoming smile for him, and their conversations at dinner and on outings had been full of humor and wit. It was only occasionally that her eyes shot fire; for the most part they had become friends.

Friendship was all right for the moment, but Dev knew now that he wanted Jena's love. With time he thought she could learn to love him with the same mindless joy that he felt. He wanted her face to light up when he entered the room. He wanted to see the banked fires of passion smoldering in her eyes. Most of all, he wanted to regularize their marriage, so they could work toward a deeper relationship.

If he confessed his love for her, they could call an immediate end to this ridiculous wager. He could just picture the expression in her eyes when he told her he adored her and would accept the marriage. As Dev stared into the fire, the vision of Jena shifted, dissolving and re-forming into the face of his mother. He jerked to his feet, the glass falling to the carpet unnoticed as he paced the room in agitation.

Never could he tell Jena he loved her! He had

sworn as a child that he would never permit a woman to control him as his father had been controlled. His mother had used the knowledge of his father's love more skillfully than a wielded knife to cut away his father's self-respect and pride. No woman would ever have that power over him, Dev vowed.

Stalking to the window, Dev stared down at the darkened street. He ached with the knowledge that despite his fear of Jena's control, he wanted her. Somehow he had to get her to cancel the wager. He could not forfeit without her suspecting the reasons. Yet she could not win. He had stacked the cards against her.

She could win if I let her. Dev smiled slyly at his reflection in the window. He could not tell her he loved her. After all, he had his pride. If she won the wager, he had agreed to acknowledge the marriage. So be it. He would help her to win. The total irony of the plan did not disconcert him. Instead, he condemned himself for taking advantage of her by offering such a paltry allowance. That was the crucial point where she could lose the wager. He would have to plan carefully so that her money lasted.

God in Heaven! He had forgotten about the party!

The duke had demanded Jena make her bow to society. Originally Dev had soothed his grandfather by explaining that he had promised his wife a month without social obligations. Once the month had passed, the letters from the old man increased in frequency and vituperation. In the light of his newfound wisdom, Dev admitted that he had put off the inevitable confrontation because of his fears for Jena.

Dev knew the kind of scrutiny Jena would be under when he introduced her to society. The unusual speed of their marriage would make the high-toned

143

tabbies twice as careful before giving his new wife the nod of acceptance. Every movement, every word, and every gesture of Jena's would be examined for flaws, and the slightest error in judgment would sink her beyond recall. Although Jena had been able to run his household, nothing could prepare her for the responsibilities of a *ton* party. The slightest breach of etiquette would be noted and condemned by the guests. Dev shuddered to think what society would make of the motley crew of servants and their bizarre livery.

Slowly a plan formulated in Dev's mind. The rich and privileged adored the outrageous as long as it fell within certain boundaries. If he treated the matter of the servants with a humorously raised eyebrow, so, too, would society. Could the sophisticated Lord Devereaux Havenhurst, Viscount Badderley, and heir to the Duke of Wayfield be playing a little joke? they would ask.

It was a risk, of course, Dev realized. He would have to trust that he had enough influence to carry it off. He hoped the servants could play their parts so that the guests would only be appalled by their looks, not their efficiency. Up to this point they had performed their duties to perfection. If he were a wagering man, Dev thought in amusement, he would bet they would come up to snuff.

Would Jena be able to hold her own among the *ton*? Her antecedents aside, she had grace, wit, and manners enough to charm the highest sticklers. If he was beside her, he could ease any awkwardness. He had enough address to put down any threats to her acceptance. His real worry was that her allowance would permit few of the lavish touches that would guarantee the success of the party. All he could do was to suggest the party, limit the guest list, and then trust to her ingenuity. No matter

144

what she did, he would treat it as the expected arrangement. Society would take its cue from him.

The logs in the fireplace shifted as the fire began to die out. Dev untied his dressing gown and threw it on the edge of the bed. Under the covers, he settled against the pillows as his thoughts shifted drowsily. He had never realized how big and empty his bed was. Soon, he promised, grinning up at the canopy.

He imagined the joy he would take having Jena enclosed within the bed curtains. Her lush body would writhe in eagerness for his kisses. His fingers would plunge into the mass of silken curls and he would glory in the adoration of her eyes. She would feel confident in her love and be grateful that he had honored his part of the bargain. He shifted restlessly, wondering why the thought of her gratitude was not more exhilarating. He was giving up much to make her his bride in reality as well as name.

Damn the contrary wench! Dev railed. Could she not be satisfied with what he could give her? How dare she look at him with reproach in her beautiful gray eyes! Typical of women. They were all greed. He would just have to be strong. Confessing his love would weaken his position. Love could not demand this final surrender.

Chapter Eleven

"Watch your step, Miss Jena," Martine cautioned as he handed her out of the carriage. "No need to rush your fences."

Jena grinned saucily at the old gypsy. She slowed her pace across the stable yard, taking time to notice the improvements that had been made since her last visit. The place glistened with new paint, and the freshly washed windows sparkled in the late afternoon sunlight. She raised an eyebrow in inquiry at the line of daisies that edged the sides of the main stables.

Martine shrugged self-consciously. "Timothy Leary's wife thought a touch of color might not be amiss." He sniffed in denial that such frivolous additions should have come on his orders.

"The girl's got sense. Show's a pride in our efforts," Jena said. "I gather Timothy is working out well."

"Lad's got an eye for horseflesh and a way with them as well." Despite the gruff tone, Martine's words were high praise.

Jena's heart was filled to bursting as she entered the stables. Although it was a far cry from the sumptuous arrangements in her father's time, the stud farm was very definitely a going concern.

Every Wednesday when she visited, there were additions and improvements to the place. There was an air of competence and experience that permeated the establishment, from the scrubbed oak floors to the polished nameplates on the stalls.

She and Martine had drawn up a list of priorities; their emphasis had been the acquiring of prime stock. With the limited funds available, they were aware many improvements would have to be put off. One thing they had not taken into consideration was the joy the tenants would feel at the reopening of the stud and the return of the well-respected Miss Christie. Each of the tenants had supported their effort through labor in their off hours by painting and repairs or by homegrown provisions for Martine and the other stud workers. This enabled Martine to focus entirely on purchasing mares and stallions to build up the stud.

For Jena the change in Martine filled her with happiness. It was hard to recall the hopeless, disheveled wretch that she had found in the back of Worley Livery. The old gypsy's clothes were almost dandified in their cleanliness, and she twitted him on the fact that there was a hint of bay rum that wafted up from the Belcher scarf knotted at his neck. His thick thatch of gray hair was trimmed short, not for fashion, but for ease of care. It still had a tendency to shoot forward, a complement to the heavy eyebrows bristling above twinkling eyes. Martine strode through the stables, jabbing with his stout walking stick to punctuate his explanations. His body radiated a confidence and pride that occasionally brought tears to her eyes.

Jena remembered clearly her first visit after Martine had taken over the running of the stud. She had been quaking with nervousness, but her chin was raised determinedly as he ushered her into the office. Jena waited impassively while one of the footmen placed a large box on the desk. Martine eyed her suspiciously as he closed the door after the departing servant and jammed his thumbs into the waistband of his buckskins. The mulish expression on his face augured ill for her enterprise.

"What is it?" Martine growled.

"It's a new leg."

The gypsy's head snapped up, and a blaze of fury shot from his eyes. Jena did not react, holding his eyes with a bored expression. He hated her for mentioning the forbidden subject. Although he had outwardly improved, Jena knew that the loss of his leg was far more crippling mentally than physically. The awkwardness of the peg leg only emphasized his handicap.

"I've work to do," Martine snapped, stumping toward the door.

"Get back here, you old reprobate," Jena shouted. She wanted to reach out and touch him, but held herself still with an iron control. "I've an investment to consider. I need you to work at peak capacity."

"I'm mobile enough," Martine said, his back stiff with resentment. "I do the job you hired me for as best I can."

Jena refused to acknowledge the self-pitying tone. "It's called an articulated leg. Invented by a Dr. Pott. The Earl of Uxbridge, Wellington's second in command, lost his leg. A ball took it at Waterloo. He tried a peg at first but said he couldn't get out and about the way he was used to. He tried several models, I gather, before he settled on this design called the Pott's Leg. I overheard two ladies talking about it in the park."

"Eavesdropping, huh!" the gypsy snorted, turning to face Jena. His face was shuttered, the muscles taut along his jawline. There was a sag to his shoulder, as though he had lost a battle of his own. "Let's have a look at it."

With the knob of his cane, he flipped back the cover of the box. Cautiously he folded back the nest of papers as if expecting something loathsome to leap out at him. When he had laid bare the contents, a slight whistle of air escaped his pursed lips.

The wooden appliance was shaped like a real leg, complete with knee, ankle, foot, and toes. The intriguing part was that each segment of the leg possessed a movable joint. Even the toes had mobility. It was eerie in the attention to detail that gave it such a lifelike appearance.

"It's not perfect, Martine, but it's bound to give you more agility," Jena said briskly. "It's wood and leather. The straps in front of the knee joint hold your trouser leg free of the mechanism."

"Newfangled ideas!" he scoffed. "Probably break under pressure."

Gnarled fingers lifted the leg, examining the way the knee flexed. His face was blank, but there was a reverence to his touch that told Jena all she needed to know. Slowly the muscles along her shoulders relaxed. After a minute examination, Martine carefully restored the leg to the box. Without a word, he stumped to the door, holding it open for Jena. He gave her a tour of the stables as though nothing had occurred to interrupt their normal routine.

The following Wednesday, Martine was standing outside the stables as Jena's carriage approached. He was wearing new buckskins, each trouser leg falling straight to the tops of polished boots. Jena blinked rapidly to hold back her tears when she perceived the change in the old man's face. It was lit with pride, self-respect and humor. Martine, the

149

man she had loved as a child, had returned. Neither mentioned the leg. Their eyes touched and there was little need of words.

"Your head's in the clouds, lass," Martine grumbled, bringing Jena's thoughts back to the present. "Are you worrying about something?"

"Beg pardon, Martine," she said, patting his sleeve in apology. "Must be the lovely spring day. Or the dawdling pace. I'm champing at the bit to see the newest addition."

"And well you might," he crowed. He moved ahead of her, slowing as he approached a stall separated from the others. Reaching for the brass handle, he opened the door and stepped back to give Jena a good view. "This is Alastor."

The black stallion jerked up his head, and his tail whipped against his rump. He blew sharply through his nostrils and arched his neck, surveying the intruders. Jena caught her breath as her eyes caressed the satiny coat over rippling muscles. He was magnificent. She remained motionless as the black approached, snuffling her shoulder, then brushing down the front of her dress.

"Gentle as a newborn," Martine whispered beside her.

"Not likely, you old fake," Jena chuckled as the stallion attempted to nip her fingers. "He's a beauty all right."

"Glad you didn't see him when he arrived." Martine cuffed the horse firmly when the black bared his teeth. He pulled Jena back, closing the half door for good measure. "I sent Timothy up north to fetch him. Knew if I showed my face, the price would go up. As it was, we got him for a pittance. He was a sorry sight when he got here. Ill fed and poorly groomed. A week of good care has him back in fighting condition."

150

"When will he be ready?"

"Want to feed him up for another week. Plenty of care. Give him back a sense of himself," Martine said gruffly, patting the neck of the stallion.

"And you think he'll be successful at stud?" Jena asked, comfortable with the plain speaking of the stables. This was the world she had grown up in, and she treated the subject matter-of-factly.

"It's a risk, Miss Jena, as I warned you." Martine's teeth worried his bottom lip, and his eyes were focused intently on the black. "When he was racing, Alastor was considered a wonder horse. He had speed and stamina combined with a fierce competitive spirit. I saw him race twice and I couldn't take my eyes off of him, he was that incredible. I've never gotten over the experience, and so I've kept tabs on him through the years. He was sold to stud four years ago for a bleeding fortune. Your father would have bought him, but he was already in River Tick. It near broke my heart when word filtered down that he was a failure at stud."

"Who bought him?" Jena asked.

"Place in Ireland called Thatches, run by Jamie MacNamara, an impatient boozer of a man. He wants a quick turnout for any outlay of gold. Efficient enough, but treats all the horses the same. Unfortunately, like humans, each one is different."

Martine gave the stallion a final slap on the neck and led Jena back through the compound toward his office. His head was bent, his mind still concentrated on the problems of Alastor.

"When your father was alive, I had dealings with MacNamara. Remember Sly Lady? Took her up to Ireland to be serviced by Polyx. Stayed at the stud for a couple of months. After she dropped her foal, I had plenty of time to look round the establishment before she came into season again. It's a tremendous layout. It's located around a wide, flat expanse of springy turf. MacNamara makes good use of his land. Got a vast herd of sheep that wander the area. Makes a good living out of them, too."

Jena was caught up in the rambling story, listening without interruption. She had learned from experience it was pointless to rush the man; eventually he would come to the point of the narrative.

"One day I was walking Sly Lady. I was worried about her because she didn't seem to be thriving. Didn't want her served by the stallion if she was ailing. She was getting the same care as she would at the home farm, but her eyes were dull and she was generally listless. Her foal was doing well, but it seemed to me something about the farm disagreed with Lady."

"A change of feed?" Jena suggested.

"No. I'd brought what she would need from Dunton." The old man ushered her into the office. He smiled at the waiting tea tray and poured her the customary mug of tea before he continued. "Then I noticed that Sly Lady was walking differently. Each step was hesitant, as though she misliked the feel of the turf. From then on I walked her only on hard-packed dirt. Her condition improved immediately. To this day I don't know whether it was the feel of the turf or something to do with the sheep. But it's ever been in my mind, and when I heard about Alastor I began to wonder."

Jena sipped her tea, studying Martine's weathered face. There was a suspicious twinkle in his eyes that belied the mournful expression he wore.

"Out with it, man," Jena said.

"When Timothy went north to buy Alastor, I described what to look for. The black had the same dull eye and listless manner as Sly Lady. But more to the point, when the stallion walked on the turf, his steps were hesitant, almost mincing."

"He's thriving now," Jena said, unwilling to place too much hope in Martine's theory. "If he's a success at stud, he'll be the making of the place."

"That's what I'm counting on," Martine said. "We'll know this time next week."

Jena skipped down the stairs, smiling at the thought that she would never dare comport herself so freely if Lamb had been in attendance. She enjoyed Wednesdays with all the servants away. She felt free of the responsibility of her position. The day had fallen into a pattern, with her visit to the stud in the afternoon and then a long, lazy evening of reading.

Her heels clicked lightly on the marble floor as she headed for the library to choose a book. She crossed to the shelves beneath the loft, humming lightly under her breath. Her fingers skipped across the leather spines as her eyes searched for something of interest. She bit her lip, uncertain of her choice.

"Poetry is to your left," said a deep voice from behind her.

Jena whirled, her hands pressed to her bosom, where the pounding of her heart threatened to burst through her chest. She blinked rapidly at the grinning viscount, who was slouched comfortably in a deep chair beside the window.

"What are you doing here?"

"Sorry, my dear," Dev drawled, getting to his feet. "I apologize for startling you, but after all, I do live here."

"But Lamb told me you were going to your club," she accused.

"For once the redoubtable Lamb is in error. Actually, I was at my club, but the company was boring. I thought I would be happier before my own fire. That is, if I had a fire." He stared at the unlighted fireplace.

"I'm sorry," Jena said, wriggling in discomfort. "The servants should be back soon, and then someone could light it."

"I am not totally incompetent, my dear," Dev said. "If I really required a fire, I suspect I might be able to manage."

"Of course," Jena said.

"Won't you join me? I've been hoping for a chance to speak with you."

Jena hesitated. A feeling of uneasiness crept into her consciousness as she stared at her husband. There was something different about the man. An air about him of controlled excitement that she immediately distrusted. However, short of being rude, she could hardly deny such a simple request. And besides, a voice announced in her head, you enjoy his company. Ducking so he would not see the flush of color rising to her cheeks, Jena seated herself on the settee across from his chair.

"Where do you go on Wednesdays?" Dev asked.

"What?" Jena's eyes widened at the question.

"I wondered where you went on the servants' day off." Dev was surprised at the guilty start of the girl at his idle question. He took note of the slender hands gripped tightly together in her lap, and his interest was piqued.

"N-Nanny and I go for a drive," Jena stammered.

"Doesn't John Coachman have the day off?" Dev asked. He kept his expression only politely inquiring, but he was more and more mystified by her behavior.

"No. I mean, yes." She tried to bring her nerves under control by taking a deep breath. "John drives us around and then he takes his afternoon off," she finished triumphantly.

"Wonder where he goes," Dev mused, his voice noncommital. Jena was a terrible liar, he thought in amusement. Her eyes took on a hunted quality that tipped her hand. He would definitely have to give this development some thought. "Did you find a book?"

The quick change of subject flustered Jena, and once more she stumbled over her words. "N-no. I couldn't decide."

"Perhaps I might suggest something."

Dev got out of his chair and strolled to the bookshelves. Jena pressed her back against the cushions of the settee. She had an overwhelming urge to giggle like the veriest schoolroom miss. If only Dev knew where all the servants went on their day off, his eyes would take on that glazed look she remembered from the first time he had seen the ragtag group.

It had been Martine's idea originally. He told her that the money she could put into the stud was not sufficient. In order to make the breeding farm a viable establishment, they needed twice, perhaps three times the amount. At her dismay his eyes had crinkled and he suggested a plan to increase their purse.

The servants had been hired through contacts at the various racecourses, breeding farms, and training stables. There was nothing that went on in the horse world that at least one of her staff did not know. Martine intended to use this network to reinvest the money by placing knowledgeable bets on match races. Wednesday the servants dispersed to pick up the racing gossip and report everything back to Lamb. The butler then placed the bets, leaning heavily on his experience as a tout. In the first month, despite one nasty loss, they had tripled the money for the stud. In the second month, they had done even better.

"Here you are, Jena."

She jumped as Dev extended a book for her examination. Without glancing at the cover, she grasped it and placed it on the settee beside her. She eyed him warily, wondering at his solicitous behavior.

"You said you wanted to speak to me," Jena said, wanting to end the interview until she had time to gather her wits about her.

"Ah, yes," Dev said, reseating himself. He crossed his long legs and placed one shining booted foot on top of his other knee. "I thought it time for you to make your bow to society. I have been sorely remiss in my duties. But I mean to make up for any lapse in my responsibilities to my wife."

What was the bloody man up to? Jena muttered inelegantly, but she kept her voice noncommital when she spoke. "What exactly did you have in mind, Devereaux?"

"It was my intention to ask you, my dear. Thought it might be time for a party of some kind. Nothing lavish, mind you." He wished he had given some thought to the least expensive entertainment they might provide. "Perhaps a Venetian breakfast or a musicale. Just a small, select gathering."

So that's what he's planning, Jena thought. A select gathering indeed. Probably the starchiest tabbies in society. Dev must be a poor gamester to so overplay his hand. His overly solicitous concern for her and then his ludicrous suggestions were to throw her off the scent. She knew the deep game he was playing. He hoped to embarrass her in front of the *ton* in order to win the wager. She was surprised at the hurt she felt at such an underhanded ploy.

"That sounds perfectly lovely, Dev," Jena agreed. "Had you a date in mind?"

"Would three weeks be short notice?"

"I suspect I could manage," Jena answered cautiously, her mind busy with conjectures. She knew she would have to do everything on a grand scale or he would use the paltriness of the affair to win the wager. She sighed at his cleverness. Unless she was extremely inventive, the party would be beyond her budget. Looking up, she found Dev watching her intently. He was probably hoping she would throw up her hands in defeat. Never! At least, not without a fight.

"I think a ball would be nice," Jena said.

"Really, my dear, no need to go to extremes," Dev said. "Something simpler would do just as well."

The slight agitation in his voice convinced Jena of his guilt. No doubt he feared she would humiliate him in front of his friends. The arrogant boor, she fumed. Just for that she would host a spectacular, glittering affair, if it took every penny in her purse! Anger blinded her to the fact that she could not afford such a gesture.

"I think not, milord." Jena's tone was brittle. "Only a ball would be suitable to introduce the wife of a viscount to the *ton*."

"Do you think you can manage?" Dev asked worriedly. "I would be more than happy to help in any way I can."

I'm sure you would, Jena muttered. Aloud she said, "If you would be so kind as to take care of the invitations, I will handle the rest."

Damn and blast, Dev cursed. He had mismanaged the whole conversation. He had seen the suspicion in Jena's eyes but had bulled his way ahead. Now in her wariness, the contrary wench had boxed

157

herself into a corner. A ball would cost the earth! Didn't she want to win the wager?

Silence filled the room as both occupants were busily reviewing their conversation. Their faces were expressionless, but the restlessness of their eyes indicated the busy calculations of their minds. Apparently their thoughts took approximately the same time, because abruptly both stood up, startled to discover themselves face-to-face.

Dev stared down at Jena, noting the color high on her cheeks. She was so close that he could see the pulse fluttering in her neck. His eyes dropped to the low neckline of her dress, where her soft bosom rose and fell with her rapid breathing. Slowly Dev raised his hand.

When he touched her, Jena thought she might swoon. His fingers stroked her cheek. Her heart pounded in her ears. She knew she should break away, but her own cravings for Dev's touch were in complete control of her will. Her eyes fluttered closed as Dev's face hovered above her, and she waited eagerly for the touch of his lips. And then he was kissing her. His lips were warm, pressing firmly against her trembling mouth. His hands moved, one cupping the back of her head, the other holding her body in a close embrace.

Jena liked the feel of Dev's kiss. It was gentle, sending delightful sensations through her body. Her hands came up; she knew she should push him away. She touched his chest and felt his start of surprise. Then of their own volition, her hands continued upward to circle his neck.

Dev groaned and his mouth shifted. His senses were inflamed and he deepened his kiss. Her shuddering moan drove him onward and his tongue forced entry as his hands moved on her body. He had known what it would be like to touch her. Lush curves. Creamy skin. It was all there beneath his caressing fingers. His fingers fumbled at the buttons of her bodice, his knuckles grazing the silken valley of her breasts.

It was this contact that broke through Dev's erotic frenzy. The skin of her breasts was satiny, untouched to his overheated mind. He pictured Jena as he saw her now and knew without reason or doubt that she was an innocent. She might be an actress, but her responses told him she had never known a man. Happiness filled him that he would be the one to teach her the joys of love. He would have to woo her slowly. He could not take her, like some serving wench, on the floor of the library. Ashamed of himself, he pushed her away.

Jena staggered when Dev broke the embrace. In an instant she came to her senses, whirling away from his hands when he reached out to steady her. She raised a fist, wanting to strike him, then pressed it to her swollen mouth and ran from the library. She was grateful for the absence of the servants as she raced up the stairs to her bedroom. Flinging herself across the bed, she burst into tears, pounding the pillows with her fists in her outburst of emotion.

What had come over her? She had behaved like a shameless wanton. She had not only accepted Dev's embrace, but she had reveled in it. But even as the silent tears rolled down her face, Jena knew what had prompted her loss of control. She had fallen in love with her husband.

Jena had agreed to the incredible marriage out of her desperate need for financial security. In order to save her name and reputation she had entered into the infamous wager with Dev. It had never occurred to her that she could ever fall in love with him. In the beginning she had hated him.

She found him arrogant, underhanded, rude, and prideful. Slowly as they spent more time together, she discovered another side to him and found enjoyment, even friendship, in his company. At some time that friendship had turned into love.

Pushing herself upright, Jena wiped her eyes with the back of her hands. The agonized lines of her face smoothed out as she hardened her heart in decision. She had to win the wager. She had been determined to win before, but then she was only risking financial ruin. Now she risked the loss of everything that was important in her life. She wanted desperately to remain married to Dev.

Jena knew that Dev desired her; the scene in the library proved that. With time, his passion could be channeled into love. Once he accepted the marriage, he would look at her more closely and realize the kind of person she was. He would grow to love her, Jena reasoned. I'll make him love me! But deep in her heart, she wondered if her hopes and desires would ever be fulfilled.

Chapter Twelve

"God in Heaven!" Jena crumbled the letter in her hand and pressed her fist to her chest. She tried to force down the rising panic that threatened to engulf her.

"What is it, child?" Nanny asked, frightened at the white face of her charge.

"Alastor and two of the mares are sick." Jena's tone was lifeless as she delivered this disheartening news. Her mind churned with the contents of Martine's letter, which had been delivered by Lamb at first light. Thank heavens it was Wednesday, when she normally visited the stud. She would just start earlier than usual. "Tell Lamb we'll be leaving in an hour, Nanny. And let Cook know that we will want something to eat beforehand."

Nanny bustled out the door as Jena kicked back the bedclothes. By the time the old woman had returned with her breakfast tray, Jena was already buttoning the short jacket of a forest-green velvet traveling dress. The sleeves of the jacket were edged in softest sable, matching the trim along the edge of the skirt. With little regard for her hair, Jena plunked the green velvet bonnet on her head, rescuing the dangling ribbons from falling into her cup of tea. She stuffed her feet into her half boots while

161

she munched a scone, her mind busy with worries over the stud.

She should have suspected that things were going too well. Martine had warned her that it was a risky enterprise, and thus far their luck had held. Even though she was determined to win the wager, she wanted the stud farm to succeed because so many people were counting on it. She had only two more weeks before the deadline of the wager. But no matter whether she won or lost, she wanted the stud to survive.

Cramming the last of the scone in her mouth, she scooped up her gloves and her reticule and started out the door. Her mind was preoccupied as she descended the stairs so that she did not see Dev until she was almost upon him. Tottering on the edge of the last step, she trembled when his large hand shot out to steady her.

"It seems much too early for such precipitous haste, milady," Dev drawled. His eyebrow raised as his wife's color faded and then rushed back to paint two spots of color high on her cheekbones. She looked particularly stunning, her black hair striking against the deep green tones of her dress. "Why, Jena, you seem positively breathless."

"It was only the surprise," she said, her eyes faltering beneath the steady cobalt stare. "I did not see you, as I fear I was busy with my own thoughts."

"I was just going out for a morning ride in the park. And where are you off to at such an unconscionable hour?"

"Uh, shopping. I mean, a-a fitting," she stammered.

Dev did not miss the hunted look in Jena's eyes or the stiffness of her figure. She truly was a rotten

162

liar. She should have thought of a more plausible story than such an obvious bouncer.

"How boring for you," Dev said politely. "Permit me."

He took the dangling velvet ribbons in his hands and tied a bow close to her right ear. The back of his hand grazed her soft white throat, and the touch jolted him with a wild surge of desire. She was so close and he stared into her face, his eyes caressing the white expanse of her brow and the feathering lashes that trembled like butterflys against her flushed cheek. Her nostrils were slightly flared, like an animal sensing danger. With the knuckles of his fist he nudged beneath her chin until her pouting mouth was raised to his.

At the touch of Dev's lips, a weakness invaded the depths of her body. Jena felt her pulses leap, and the normal sounds of the morning faded away into a whirling vortex. This was not the passionate, consuming kiss she had experienced in the library. Instead it was a sweet caress, all the more powerful for its tenderness. She knew the gentle touch of his lips had marked her soul for all eternity.

"Your carriage is ready, Lady Havenhurst."

Lamb's harsh whisper tore across Dev's already overheated nerves. He swung around, prepared to give the man a well-deserved set-down. His mouth opened and his eyes flashed dangerously until he felt the soft touch of Jena's leather glove on his wrist.

"Your pardon, Devereaux," she said. "I do not like to leave the horses standing."

The tiny figure in green velvet stepped in front of Dev, effectively blocking him from the butler. Lamb, his lantern-jawed face impassive, listened to Jena's quietly spoken orders as he walked her to the door. Dev stood transfixed until the sharp click of the door brought him back to life. Then forcing a look of bored indifference to blanket his face, he strolled to the door.

"Please tell her ladyship I will not be back for lunch," Dev said to the narrow-eyed butler.

Dev stood on the top step of the town house, his attention concentrated on the drawing on of his beige riding gloves. Out of the corner of his eye he watched the progress of Jena's carriage as it lumbered up the street to disappear around the bend in the road. Conscious of the ominous figure of Lamb hovering in the open doorway, Dev ambled down the stairs at a measured tread. He patted the deep chest of his bay, then grasped the reins and accepted a leg up from the footman. As though he had nothing on his mind but his attire, he corrected the tilt of his hat and brushed down the front of his dark brown riding jacket. Satisfied at last, he signed to the footman to step away from Killian's head, and kneed the horse into a steady trot down the street. Only after he was out of sight of the town house did he pick up the pace of the stallion until he once more had the carriage in sight.

"Steady, Killian," Dev said, patting the eager bay's neck. "We best keep back until we see where the lady is heading."

Dev had become extremely curious over Jena's disappearance every Wednesday. A casual questioning of the servants had elicited nothing but blank stares. Either they did not know or, more probably, they would not say. At first Dev had wondered if it was possible that she was seeing another man. He was shocked at the blinding rage he had felt at her duplicity. Once he had calmed down he realized that Jena was not the kind of woman who would ever consider a clandestine affair. No matter the unusual conditions of their marriage, Jena was not a woman of loose morals. She would be horrified at the mere thought of infidelity.

However, the puzzle of her Wednesday activities remained. He intended to follow her carriage until he discovered where she was going. He did not like the idea of spying on his own wife, but he consoled himself with the thought that he was merely satisfying his curiosity.

As the carriage drove out of London, Jena relaxed against the squabs and chatted quietly to Nanny. When they reached the turnpike, the old woman dozed and Jena's thoughts flew ahead to Dunton Stud. Martine's letter had not been specific, only alerting her to the fact that Alastor and two of the mares had become ill. She prayed neither one of the mares was in foal.

As the wheels of the carriage ate up the miles, Jena thought about the possibility that all their planning might be ruined. After Alastor had been pronounced strong enough to be put to stud, she and Martine had debated their best course of action. They both knew the preferred time to breed was February so that the spring-born colt would have the benefit of the long summer weather to build up its strength. Martine was of the opinion that breeding the mares in the summer and early fall would give them an advantage of the warm summer sun at the end of the pregnancy, when the mare's strength might be at a low ebb. They decided finally to breed the stallion immediately so that if the mares held to service, they could assure the racing trainers that the black was no longer a failure at stud.

They had placed all their hopes on Alastor. His pedigree would command high stud fees once it could be shown that he was a proven breeder. His foals would sell at top prices. By next spring, or summer at the least, the stud could conceivably show a profit. Unless the mares slipped their foals or, worst of all, Alastor died.

By the time Jena's carriage pulled into the stable yard she was near-frenzied. She stepped down, taking an invigorating breath of the earthy June air. A mask of serenity slid over her face and she walked briskly but unhurriedly into the stables. She suspected that it was her imagination, but an air of depression seemed to hang like a pall over the place. It took her several minutes before she found Martine, Timothy, and the rest of the grooms loitering disconsolately outside Alastor's stall. Anxious faces acknowledged her presence as she stepped forward to examine the black.

The proud stallion was a pathetic picture. He moved listlessly within the stall. He carried his head low, and when he raised it, his eyes were dull and lackluster. A watery discharge ran from his nose, and from time to time he rubbed his neck against the top edge of the half door. When Jena turned, Martine began to speak without delay.

"He went off his feed a few days ago. Now his body is overheating and his heart rate is too rapid. More worrisome is the swelling along his jawline."

Jena closed her eyes as memory engulfed her. She had been eight years old when there was an outbreak of what her father called strangles at Dunton. The disease had swept through the stud like wildfire, and at the end they had lost three stallions and seven brood mares. She could remember her hollow-eyed father dragging himself into the house at the end of each day as the toll mounted. He had not known how to stop or cure the disease. Martine had been there then, and she knew without asking that he suspected the dread disease had struck again. If true, only a miracle could save the stud.

Jena sensed Dev's presence even before she opened her eyes. He was standing directly in front of her, his expression unreadable. She did not question how he had found her. She was filled with a feeling of relief for his calm attendance. Her eyes searched his steady blue gaze and she drew strength from him, as he had intended. It did not seem unnatural that she should turn to him in her time of trouble.

"Welcome to Dunton Stud, Lord Havenhurst."

Although Jena's words were formal, her gray eyes were warm with gratitude. She extended her hand and Dev enfolded it between both of his. Quickly she introduced him to the circle of men and then let Martine briefly describe the situation. At first the old gypsy was hostile, but he dropped his antagonism when Dev's questions showed both knowledge and concern.

"I had a similar outbreak last year," Dev said, his eyes reflecting the remembered horror. "It was the first time that we'd had any success in fighting the disease. We kept our losses to a minimum," he finished tersely.

"What do you suggest, sir?" Martine asked.

For the first time since Jena had awakened to the disastrous news, she felt a small bubble of amusement. Dev must have really impressed the crotchety old man. Martine thought that titles should be earned, not bestowed at birth. She wondered how long it would take before Dev became milord.

"Well, Martine, I'm no expert on this," Dev began. "As near as I can figure, this disease travels from one horse to the other, but I have no idea how it moves. We'll start with the horses that show no signs of illness. We'll bathe each horse and then hobble it in the pasture in the sun. There is no breeze, so they should take no injury from the dousing. Keep all the horses well separated." Dev's deep voice was firm, and the men never took their eyes off him as he issued orders. "Once the stables are cleared, we will muck out all the stalls and burn the bedding. Then we'll wash down everything. Walls, tack, tools. The lot. We'll need more hands, Martine."

"Timothy will take care of that. I'm needed here to keep an eye on you." The gypsy grinned, his eyes crinkling at Dev's sharpened gaze.

It seemed to Jena that Dev was everywhere, supervising the grooms as they washed the horses and overseeing the younger lads who were cleaning out the stalls. His quiet voice was always firm, never critical, as he gave suggestions and made additions to his original orders. He was not afraid to get into the midst of things, his coat discarded and his shirt-sleeves rolled to display his muscular arms.

Much to Nanny's dismay, Jena had changed her stylish traveling dress for a plain homespun wool she had borrowed from Timothy's wife. She worked alongside the tenant women who had offered to help. A large fire had been built and kettles of water set to boil. She carried the tack from the barn, staggering under the load. Her hands, which had returned to the softness of a pampered lady, soon were scraped raw from the tools and other implements she hauled across the yard. At noon she went in search of Dev to see if she could lure him away for something to eat. She found him standing outside Alastor's stall.

His white hair was covered with particles of straw, and his neck was ringed with dirt. Jena wondered how Weatherby would react to the ruination of his lordship's riding clothes. Aware of his furrowed brow and unfocused eyes, she placed a hand on his arm to alert him to her presence. Dev turned

168

slowly as though his mind had difficulty relinquishing his thoughts.

"I think you have a smudge of dirt on your face, my dear," Dev drawled. His grin flashed wolfishly as he leaned over to touch the skin beside her temple. His face was screwed up in concentration as he rubbed the spot, then he nodded in satisfaction.

"It will take more than simple rubbing to improve your appearance, milord."

"Cheeky wench."

"How is Alastor?" she asked. She peered over the edge of the door at the woebegone animal.

"It is my opinion that he is unaffected," Dev said, noting the light of hope that sprang quickly to Jena's eyes. "One of the things that struck me when my stables were hit was that the disease did not seem to affect the older horses. Alastor is eight. I want Martine to look at him, but I am almost convinced that he has a touch of influenza."

"What about the swelling?"

"It does not look like an abscess to me. I wonder if it might not be something stupidly simple like a bug bite of some kind."

"But that's impossible," Jena bristled. "Martine never would have made such a mistake."

"Softly, little firebrand," Dev said. He put his arm casually around her shoulder, patting her as though she were a child. "A mare was the first to become ill. She had all the signs of the disease. Then another mare took sick, and finally Alastor. Once Martine knew the sickness was in the stud, he would naturally assume that the black had the same as the other two. The symptoms were the same, and the swelling on the jaw may have been smaller than on the mares, but it was nearly conclusive evidence."

Jena suspected that Dev was correct in his assessment. She could almost picture the mounting panic as one by one the horses became ill. For Martine the disaster in her father's time would be uppermost in his mind, blinding him to anything else.

"I'll send Martine to you," Jena said. "When you've finished, there's food waiting for you."

"Now that you mention it, I do have a rather hollow feeling." Dev patted his flat stomach, smiling broadly as Jena turned to leave. "I miss the green dress, although your imitation of a dairymaid is quite fetching."

Jena stuck her tongue out at him, then went in search of Martine. When the two men joined her for a hurried plate of stew, their faces told the story well before their announcement that Alastor did indeed have influenza.

"We're taking every precaution," Martine said, "so that in his weakened condition he does not pick up anything from the other horses. We'll treat him the same as the others, but I can tell you I'm much relieved."

"So am I," Jena said, sagging wearily against the tree she was sitting under. She smiled at Dev, who was sprawled on the grass, sipping a mug of cider. He did not look the part of the elegant Lord Havenhurst, but to her mind she liked him better.

"I have another suggestion to make which I think will ease the discomfort of the sick mares," Dev said, pushing himself to a sitting position. "We'll need some old feed bags with holes in the bottom so that air can filter through. We'll line the bag with clean hay and sprinkle it with oil of eucalyptus. Then we pour boiling water over the hay and stick the mare's nose inside the bag. It acts like a medicinal steaming to help clear the horse's head."

"It's worth a try," Martine said, stroking the head of his walking stick as he stared into space.

"I think we ought to detail a boy to stay with each horse. I've seen some animals panic when their breathing is not clear. Then the lad can change the bag with some regularity."

"It would not hurt to put Alastor on the same regime," Dev said. "You'll have to watch him so that he doesn't come down with an inflammation of the lungs. This should help, or in any event, it won't hurt."

Martine cuffed Dev lightly on the shoulder and then started back to the stables. "I'll get right on it, milord," he threw over his shoulder.

"Congratulations, Dev, you have quite won Martine's heart," Jena said. She was bursting with pride at how her husband had taken over, controlling a situation that had filled her with nothing but despair.

"And yours, my dear?" Dev asked quietly, his eyes steady on her face.

Jena ignored his question, schooling her expression to a calmness she was far from feeling. "I appreciate everything you have done today, Dev. I was so frightened that my mind was quite literally frozen. How did you come to be here?"

"I followed you," he answered, grinning at her look of outrage. "I was curious as to where you went every Wednesday."

He stared at her, his face grave as his eyes searched hers. "Jena, I want to call an end to the wager. After watching you today, I wish to regularize our marriage."

Jena turned her head away so that he would not see the blaze of happiness written clearly on her face. She, too, had felt a joy in working side by side to save the horses. He had begun already to enjoy her company, and now at last he had discovered the kind of loving relationship they could have in a real

171

marriage. Nothing else explained his change of heart. Her love for him was so strong that she wanted to believe, but her mind warned her to take care.

She turned to face Dev, her face pale but wiped free of emotion. "Why, Dev?"

Now it was Dev's turn to shift uncomfortably. He had seen the quickly averted face and wondered what expression she had hidden from him. Was it joy? Triumph? He remembered how his mother had played on the emotions of his father. She had been a practiced artist, able to simulate any emotion in order to impose her will on her helpless husband. He must choose his words carefully, ever mindful of the consequences of declaring his love. He had sworn that he would never give a woman power over him, and he would be true to his promise.

"I want to end the wager because I realize now that I have done irreparable damage to your name," Dev began. "When we were married I was convinced that you were an actress. After today, there can be no doubt that you are Lady Jena Christie. I have talked to Martine and he has told me a little of Dunton's history."

"You would take the word of that old fakir?" Jena asked, her tone cutting. "I could have paid him to uphold my story."

"You could not have paid the lot of them," Dev said. "It is apparent that this was once your home and these your people."

"And if that is all true? What does it matter?"

"It matters simply that I am a gentleman and must give you the protection of my name."

Jena glared at the stiffly jutting chin of her husband, wondering how she could have ever fallen in love with such an insensitive, pompous lout. She drew her hands into fists, wanting to strike out at him but forcing herself to remain calm.

"I do not want the protection of your name!" Jena ground out between her teeth.

"Don't be a ninnyhammer!" Dev shouted, losing his temper at the contrary wench. He was giving her an opportunity to win the wager without risk. What was the matter with the woman? "Don't you want to win the wager?"

For a moment Jena wanted to scream out her answer. She didn't care a whit about the wager; all she wanted was his love. She opened her mouth and no words came forth. She moistened her dry lips and took a deep breath.

"I want to continue with the wager," Jena answered tiredly. "It is a matter of pride that I win fairly. That way you will never feel that I have taken advantage of your goodwill."

Dev searched the white face of his wife, wondering why he should feel uneasy at her response. He was still determined to help her win, but somehow he did not like the lifeless tone of her voice. Then he realized that for Jena it had been an exhausting day, and he made allowances for her inability to see how generous his offer had been. He forced himself to patience, knowing there were only two weeks until the party, and then he would have her beside him forever after.

"All right, Jena, we will continue with the wager," Dev said expansively. He picked up her hand and examined the broken nails and scratched skin from her day's endeavors. "Stay here, my dear, and relax. There's only a little more to do, and then I will see you home."

Jena watched Dev's figure as he headed back toward the stables. Her eyes burned with unshed tears and she wanted nothing more than to give in to the urge to cry. In a way, she was beyond tears. She had had such hope for their relationship, and now she realized that in winning the wager she would lose everything. She wanted Dev's love and she understood now that the only reason Dev wanted to continue the marriage was because he had compromised her. He would never love her. He would always feel that he was forced to marry her.

She had been adamant before that she would win the wager in order to continue in the marriage. Now she had another objective. She would win the wager and then inform Devereaux that she would give him an annulment. It was the only answer. She would not have Dev's love, but at least she would have her self-respect. That would have to be enough.

Chapter Thirteen

"Good Lord, Dev, we could smell your cologne clear down the street," Max said, waving a lacy handkerchief beneath his nose as he sauntered into Reggie's rooms. "I detect a trace of mint, and perhaps hmm, could it be rosemary? Although I tend to associate that with soup."

"Stubble it, clapjaw," Dev said unkindly. "Anyone wearing a mulberry jacket, white satin pantaloons, and enough lace to clothe a dozen debutantes has no call to criticize a fellow tulip of fashion."

Max was followed by a glum Dickon, obviously displeased to be dressed up in all his finery. The enormous man tugged at the buttons of his waistcoat, wondering if he had gained another stone, since it fit more snugly than the last time he had worn it. Reggie poured each of the men a drink and they ogled Dev over their glasses as they watched the finishing touches being put to his attire.

Dev glared at his friends. He was already annoyed because Jena had asked him to absent himself on the day of the party. In order to show his displeasure, he had opted to dress for the evening at Reggie's. Refusing to let the raillery of his friends put him further out of countenance, he tried to ignore them as Reggie's man Jenson helped him into his black evening coat. Although Jenson was an efficient, self-effacing valet, Dev had to admit he missed Weatherby's meandering sea stories, which always sent him off to any evening in high humor.

"Not only does he smell extremely handsome, but his clothes are a walking advertisement for Weston's art of understated elegance," Reggie pronounced in a stage whisper.

"He is truly an example to us all," Max added, saluting Dev with his glass.

"Give over," Dev said. "And more to the point, give me a drink. I have the feeling this is going to be a very long evening."

"Nervous, laddie?" Max inquired, handing him a glass.

"Yes," Dev admitted. He took a deep draft of the liquor. "God alone knows if Jena has the least idea how to go on. Even when her father was alive, she was not much involved with the country set. They did not have the money to entertain, nor did I gather that Sir George was interested in much beyond the stud. I offered to help to plan the evening, but Jena turned down any assistance."

Dev accepted Max's quick smile of sympathy as he threw himself into an easy chair. He suspected that his longtime friend had tipped to his difficulties ages ago, but at least Max had refrained from any caustic remarks at his expense.

"Nobody would miss us if we didn't show up this evening," Dickon said as though he were continuing a conversation.

"Poor Dickon, it has been a difficult time for you. But never fear, old son," Dev commiserated. "Even you will approve of our cook's expertise."

"Dickon does have a point," Reggie said. "It has occurred to me that we may be persona non grata. I cannot believe that your wife will be best pleased to see our three sunshiny faces. As you recall, the last time we met was hardly a source of great rejoicing."

Dev grimaced in remembrance of the evening. "Can it really be almost three months ago?"

"It seems longer," Dickon said morosely. "The wager's almost up, and then things can get back to normal."

"What have you planned for this evening?" Reggie asked eagerly. "How will you sabotage the ball without looking like a complete jackass?"

"I have nothing planned," Dev said, his drawling voice filled with boredom.

"What?" Reggie looked horrified. There was silence in the room as all eyes goggled at Dev, who looked totally unconcerned. Reggie coughed several times, then gathered his courage. "I say, Dev, I have noted of late that you have not made the least push to win the wager."

"It would almost appear that you are hoping your wife will win," Max added.

"The devil you say!" Dickon spluttered. "Dev wouldn't do that to us."

Dev shifted uncomfortably in his chair, his attention focused on his empty glass. Silence hung heavily in the room, and finally he raised his head and stared abashedly at his friends.

"I hate to disappoint you, gentlemen, but I have to admit I am hoping that Jena will win."

A chorus of groans greeted Dev's words, but he noticed that Max did not appear surprised. The face beneath the well-coiffed head of hair wore an approving grin, and Dev felt his own mouth widen in response.

"I knew something awful was going to happen," Dickon said. Both hands gripped the front of his waistcoat. "I've had this gnawing feeling all day."

177

"That's hunger, cuz," Reggie said. "This is serious. I can't believe that you will just forfeit, Dev."

"I'm not forfeiting," he replied. "I'm letting her win. That's entirely different."

"Why?" Reggie's voice was clearly puzzled. "Are you saying that you like being married?"

"To be perfectly honest, I have not found it to be a particularly onerous task." Dev sounded surprised and a little smug. "As you know, I fought parson's mousetrap for years, but I find that being married to Jena is not at all boring."

"I still don't understand," Reggie said.

"What a waste of time," Dickon said. "Here we've spent three months trying to help you defeat the woman, and now you've decided to just tamely give up."

"You have all stood by me admirably in this unsettling time, and I appreciate it beyond words. When you see Jena this evening I think you will begin to understand why I have come to this decision." Dev stood, solemnly shaking the hand of each of the men. "I will see you later. I am off now to lend support where I can, in hopes that the evening will be a success."

"Good evening, Lord Havenhurst," Lamb rasped.

Dev's eyes opened wide at the startling attire of his butler, and for a moment words failed him. In addition to the usual bright yellow frock coat, a black sash circled Lamb's waist out of which stuck a wide-bladed knife that gleamed wickedly in the light from the chandelier. On his head the man was wearing a shoulder-length white curled wig, a tricorn hat, and a black patch over one eye.

"Nice touch, the eye patch," Dev said, saluting the granite-faced butler with his cane. "It appears

178

that her ladyship has selected a pirate theme for tonight's gala event."

"Yes, milord," was the harsh response.

Dev surrendered his hat, cane, and gloves, all the time nervously eyeing the knife in Lamb's sash. He brushed down the front of his black jacket, debating the wisdom of turning his back to the man. As he fiddled with his cravat he felt a frisson of anticipation and swung around, staring up at the vision gliding down the staircase.

Dev had expected that Jena would wear something coolly elegant, but she had surprised him once again. Although her dress was obviously the work of an accomplished seamstress, there was nothing demure about its color or lines. It was a brilliant red chiffon, cut deeply at the neckline and falling in swirling, rippling tiers to the floor. She wore no jewelry, only a black velvet ribbon tied around her neck. Her black hair had been pulled tightly to the top of her head. Half of it was braided and circled the remainder of her hair, which tumbled in a silken cascade down her back. She had the look of a wild gypsy, vibrant with fire and passion.

"My God, Jena, you look magnificent!" Dev blurted out before he could stop himself.

Jena hesitated at the bottom step before taking the hand that Dev had extended. Praying that her nervousness would not betray her with an unconscious tremor, she placed her gloved hand in his. He touched it to his lips and she caught her breath, trapped by his glance, her senses expanding in his presence. She felt alive when she was near him and she wondered how she would survive without him. Wanting to break the spell between them, she reluctantly pulled her hand away.

"Good evening, Devereaux," she said quietly.

179

"Thank you for your promptness. As you can see, none of our guests have arrived."

"I hope you did not think that I would desert you at the final hour?" Dev asked, his eyes questioning.

"You have always acted the part of the gentleman," Jena said. "By the way, I appreciate your playing least-in-sight today."

"Think nothing of it, my dear," Dev said. His earlier annoyance had dissipated at the sight of her. "I knew you would have a million things to do, and my presence would only have been an inconvenience."

"In any case, Dev, it was thoughtful of you." Jena did not know why she suspected him of ulterior motives, but he was being altogether too accommodating. "Besides, I wanted to surprise you with the arrangements for this evening."

"I can see by the piquant additions to Lamb's livery that *Les Trois Arts* theater ensemble had an extensive wardrobe," Dev said. "No doubt this play was called *La Femme et Le Mal de Mer*."

"Truly inspired, milord," Jena laughed. "But quite off the mark. I believe the loose translation was: 'The Gypsy Maiden and the Pirates.' Lamb was not best pleased," she whispered. "He had his heart set on being a gypsy."

"Pirate definitely suits him better." Dev eyed the formidable butler and then followed Jena's lead down the hall toward the ballroom. "I am still convinced that the denizens of Bow Street would be happy to have Lamb in their clutches. If his intimidating figure doesn't rout the guests at the door, tonight's party might be a success."

Dev felt the slight tremor of Jena's hand on his sleeve. Although she was outwardly cool, he sensed that her nerves were strung tightly. Her debut would be difficult enough for a woman unused to society, but their secretive marriage added a possibility of scandal to the evening ahead.

"Nervous, Jena?" he asked.

"Of course not. The evening is well planned. All I need do is enjoy myself."

Jena spoke heartily, but there was a shadow of doubt in her eyes as they approached the closed doors to the ballroom. Dev wondered how he could encourage her without tipping his hand. He pursed his lips, his brows furrowed with concentration.

"Surely you are not nervous, milord?" Jena asked.

"Not really, my dear." Dev stopped before the closed door to the ballroom. He bowed to Jena as he said, "I have the utmost confidence in your abilities as an actress to play any role you desire."

Dev smiled at the blaze of anger in Jena's eyes. She was on her mettle now, prepared for the rigors of the evening ahead. He could not conceive of any of his guests not being charmed by his beautiful wife. His only worry was that the paltriness of her arrangements would be noted by the guests and considered an insult.

"Shall we go in, my dear?" Dev asked, hoping his voice did not convey any of his doubts.

He took a deep breath and then extended his arm to his wife. At a signal from Jena, two pirate-clad footmen leaped forward and wrenched open the doors to the ballroom. Dev blinked his eyes in disbelief, and slowly a grin replaced the worried look on his face.

The room had been transformed into a gypsy encampment. Instead of the usual banks of flowers, trees and shrubs lined the walls, giving the feeling of a clearing in the midst of a forest. At one end of the ballroom, there was a garishly decorated gypsy wagon. An old crone, who, Dev noted, looked suspiciously like Nanny, was enveloped in gaily patterned shawls and enthroned beside the wagon. Servants in colorful gypsy costumes roamed the forested edge of the dance floor. Instead of a formal orchestra, the musicians were also costumed, looking so much like real gypsies that Dev had little doubt that Jena had found the genuine article.

At the other end of the room, the French windows had been thrown open to the garden. Twinkling lights and tables were scattered among the flower beds. Even the buffet had been set outside and did not look out of place beside a huge campfire. Smoke from the fire drifted into the ballroom, blending with the dim lights of the candles to endow the scene with an almost magical quality.

"My congratulations, Jena," Dev said, taking both her hands. He raised them to his lips, kissing the knuckles of each hand with a laughing flourish. "You have quite outdone yourself."

Dev placed her hands on his chest, and his own hands dipped to circle her waist, pulling her into a close embrace. He was oblivious to everything but the heady perfume that rose to his nostrils and filled his head with erotic thoughts. He wanted to tell her how much she pleased him, how much joy she had brought to him with her droll inventiveness. He wanted to hold her and caress her. Most of all he wanted the evening to be over so that they could end the wager. Then she would be his forever.

"Thank you, Devereaux," she said, her breath coming in nervous little pants. "I am glad you approve."

"How could I not? It is a fitting setting for my wild gypsy bride," Dev said, his voice husky with restraint. "Your ingenuity is a constant amazement to me, madam."

Beneath his sharp scrutiny, Jena could feel the

quick wash of color that painted her cheeks. She knew she should pull her hands away but was conscious of a desire to circle Dev's neck with her arms and forget everything in the comfort of his embrace.

"I wanted the ball to be special, no matter the wager. You did not think I would embarrass you in front of your friends?" Jena asked softly. "Surely you trusted me?"

Dev's face, which had been looking at her so warmly, changed in an instant. He stared down at her, frowning darkly. Jena snatched her hands away, backing up in puzzlement. She did not understand what had wrought such a transformation, but as she opened her mouth to speak, the sounds of the first guests echoed down the hall. Dev shook his head. He stared at Jena but his eyes were blank, not really seeing her. Without a word, he held out his hand and they moved into the doorway of the ballroom.

Jena was so confused by Dev's change of manner that she had no time to be nervous. True to his word, he played the part of the doting husband, treating her with gracious charm as he introduced her to the cream of society. There was a great deal of humorous banter concerning the menacing servants and the intriguing atmosphere of the ballroom. The guests greeted Jena warmly, although she sensed curiosity and a slight wariness beneath their words. It was obvious that there had been a great deal of conjecture concerning their hurried marriage, but it seemed that with her husband beside her, society was willing to accept her.

Without doubt she had won the wager. Despite Dev's penny-pinching allowance, she had created a successful party. For the guests the evening was an unmitigated success, but for Jena there was a hollowness to the victory. The smiling figure beside her was only the shell of the man she had grown to love. When he looked at her, there was a blankness to Dev's eyes that indicated his withdrawal. Obviously the introduction of his wife to society had reminded Dev of the reality of their situation. The hopeless expression in his eyes was caused by his awareness that he would have to acknowledge the marriage. Despite her own pain, she wanted to tell him that he need not worry. She would free him; she would not keep him prisoner in a marriage without love.

It was late in the evening before Jena spotted three figures peeking nervously from behind the protective side of the gypsy wagon. For the first time since the ball had started, she felt her mouth curve into a smile of genuine amusement. Chuckling at their discomfort, Jena circled the floor until she was standing behind the trio. Arms crossed on her chest, she tapped her toe impatiently until one by one Reggie, Max, and Dickon became aware of her presence.

"Well, gentlemen, what have you to say for yourselves?" Jena attempted to keep her face serious, but her eyes twinkled at the look of amazement on the faces of the three men. "I trust that is not disapproval I read in your eyes?"

"You look considerably different than the last time we saw you," Reggie blurted out. "I mean, I did not recall—"

"What he is trying to say, milady, is that you look quite beautiful," Max interjected smoothly.

"Well said, good sir," Jena laughed. She could hardly keep her eyes off the outrageous floral waistcoat that he wore with such pride. "I would say the same of you, but I fear that you might take insult."

"Max is never insulted when you compliment his

wardrobe," Reggie said, elbowing the dandy in the ribs. "He spent more on that waistcoat than I did on my entire outfit."

"That is clearly apparent," Max said. He raised a quizzing glass, grimacing as he eyed his friend. "My tailor would surely weep if he could but see you, you oaf."

Reggie glowered at his dapper friend, and Jena hurried to interrupt. "We are all of us dressed in fine feathers. Unfortunately, when we first met, none of us were at our best." Jena turned and smiled warmly up at Dickon, who was staring at her with something like awe. "I'm truly glad that you have come this evening. I never did thank you for the bouquet of roses."

Embarrassed to be reminded of the hurried marriage ceremony, the huge man shifted uneasily. He stared down at the exquisite features of Dev's wife and wondered how they could ever have mistaken her for anything but a lady. Before he could apologize, Jena placed her hand on his sleeve and he leaned down to catch her softly spoken words.

"The buffet is in the garden, Dickon," she said. "Dev has told me that you are especially fond of lobster puffs, and they are one of Cook's specialties. No one would take it amiss if you should sample some of her offerings."

"You have surely won Dickon's loyalty forever, milady," Max said as the smiling bear of a man lumbered off in pursuit of food. "I fear we were not sure if you would greet us with any degree of warmth."

"I bear you no ill will," Jena said. "Besides, a hostess is always delighted to have handsome gentlemen to help her entertain the ladies." She laughed when the two men groaned. "Now, now. I promise not to introduce you to any quizzes. But

185

there are one or two charming girls who would be honored by your attentions."

Taking the men in tow, Jena led them to various groups around the room. Noticing the look of interest in Reggie's eyes when they lighted on a blushing girl in pink, Jena stopped to introduce the men. When it turned out that Reggie was acquainted with the girl's brother, Jena felt it was safe to drag Max away.

"Nicely done, Jena," Max applauded. "Elise Craig is just the sort of girl that Reggie will find enchanting. Those melting brown eyes might be his Waterloo."

"Are you suggesting that I would sink to matchmaking?" Jena's eyes looked guilelessly up at the dandy.

"Suggesting? No." Max shook his head sadly, but his eyes were dancing. "I would say I was outright accusing you of it. And now, what antidote have you in mind for me?"

"Matchmaking will never work with you," Jena said. "You are much too cynical to let a chance acquaintance with a lady influence you. I know you are not a hardened rake, for your eyes give you away. They are much too kind."

Max stopped, turning a raised eyebrow to the perceptive woman on his arm. "You will ruin my reputation with such remarks. What will your silence cost me, I wonder?"

Jena smiled, patting the sleeve of Max's mulberry jacket. "It will only cost a dance or two. All I ask is that you look for the girls who seem sorely lacking in partners. Men forget the absolute devastation for a girl when no one asks her to dance."

"No more, dear lady. I am already riddled with guilt." Max threw up his hands in defeat, but his smile was approving. "All right. Bring on your

186

squinty-eyed, snaggletoothed, bespeckled beauties. I will be brave."

After she left Max, the evening seemed interminable to Jena. She smiled until her cheeks ached. She chatted and danced, but she was forever conscious of Dev's sad eyes following her movements. He had danced the opening dance with her but had not asked for another. The evening was almost at an end when Jena looked up to find Dev standing in front of her. For a moment she forgot the imminent denouement of their wager, and her face lit with welcome.

"I have come to claim a boon," Dev said. "I petition for this dance, gypsy wife."

Jena trembled beneath the deep warmth in his voice. Tentatively she touched the tips of her gloved hand to the one he extended. Even such a simple act sent a shock of electricity through her body, and her breathing became ragged. The sad awareness of the ending of their relationship had permeated the evening, but now she closed her mind to everything except Dev's waiting arms. The opening strains of the waltz invaded her body and she relaxed in the embrace of the dance.

"You are to be congratulated, madam, on such a spectacular evening," Dev said. "The guests will be singing your praises tomorrow for entertaining them in such an intriguing manner. And on all sides I have heard nothing but the warmest compliments on the beauty, grace, and elegance of my wife."

"I am truly grateful that I did not shame you," Jena replied.

"You could never do that, my dear."

Jena looked up at the genuine sincerity of his words. It lifted her spirits to know that he did not take her in disgust. If things had been different,

187

she might have met him at some social function in London during her Season. Perhaps they might have met at Almack's or at Carlton House. They might have exchanged glances at the opera or the theater. They might have been introduced by friends in Hyde Park. In amusement Jena stared at the other dancers, imagining their horror if they knew the actual facts of her marriage to Dev.

"Is that a victory smile?" Dev asked.

Embarrassed at her straying attention, Jena blushed. "I'm sorry, but I was wool-gathering."

"I was just congratulating you on winning the wager."

"Oh." Jena didn't really want to think about it now. She had been enjoying the music and wanted only to drift in Dev's arms.

"Reggie and Dickon have lost faith in me. The most crushing blow of all in their eyes is the fact that I was defeated by a woman." Dev laughed down at Jena, taking the sting out of his words.

"And Max?" she said.

"He has known me since we were scruffy lads together. Sometimes I think he understands my feelings better than I do."

"I like your friends. And I am sorry that you have lost credit in their eyes. Perhaps I can make it up to them eventually." Jena wondered what they would think when she disappeared from Dev's life. She pushed away the question. "And you, sir, how do you feel about losing the wager? You can tell me the truth."

At her words, the smile on Dev's face froze and once more a bleakness crept into his expression. There was a momentary pause and then Dev laughed, the sound brittle to Jena's ears. The smile returned to his face, but it did not touch his eyes.

"The truth. How novel," he said, a curious note

in his voice. "In truth, my dear, I have always thought you would make a perfectly exquisite mistress."

Jena stiffened at the insult. She wanted to tear herself out of his arms but had neither the will nor the strength. A sheen of moisture filmed her eyes, but she would not give him the satisfaction of seeing how deeply he had hurt her. The only thing that saved her was that suddenly the music stopped. As Dev released her, she spun on her heel and exited the floor, her back straight and her chin raised proudly.

For the remainder of the evening, Jena avoided Dev. It took all her acting skill to bid a charming good night to the guests, and as soon as the last couples left, she fled to the darkest part of the garden.

Jena strolled the paths until she found a bench against the back wall and sank down gratefully on the rough stone surface. The heady smell of the flowers surrounded her, and the velvet darkness pressed down, filling her with a yearning ache. It was a night made for lovers. How different everything would be if Dev loved her as much as she loved him.

"Hiding, my dear?"

Dev's voice startled Jena and she leaped to her feet. She felt vulnerable and afraid of her own response to his nearness. She turned to run, but his hand shot out and he captured her wrist in a grip of iron. Even in the darkness she could make out his harsh features, and she wanted to cry for all that she had lost. Slowly he pulled her to him until her hands pressed against his chest. She tilted her head back to search his face, but he moved, his head blotting out all light as his mouth sought hers.

The touch of his lips was tentative, feather-light

strokes against hers. His arms surrounded her. His hands moved, touching her, pressing her to him, stroking, caressing. Her lips parted beneath the pressure of his mouth.

As though he had been waiting for her response, his kiss deepened. It was a passionate kiss, full of hunger and desire. It was not the respectful embrace of a lover but the lustful caress of a man with his mistress. Remembering Dev's words on the dance floor, Jena stiffened in the circle of his arms. For a moment sanity returned and she pushed against his chest.

"Please, Dev," Jena said. "Let me go."

"If only I could." Dev's voice was harsh in the night air.

His words cut Jena as no knife could. She could not believe that he would be so cruel. His words broke the last vestiges of the seductive spell that surrounded her, and Jena pushed away from him. She was furious that she had permitted her desire for his love to blind her to their hopeless situation. He did not love her, and she could accept nothing less. She knew he hated the fact of their marriage, but the sheer hopelessness in his voice hurt her beyond belief. There was silence in the garden, broken by the sound of their ragged breathing.

"You have won the wager, Jena," Dev said. "I will accept the marriage, as I promised."

"Thank you, Dev, but such a sacrifice is not necessary," Jena said quietly. "The wager was for three months, and there are still three more days until the time is up. Therefore, I will tell you now that I am forfeiting the wager. I want an annulment."

Chapter Fourteen

"What do you mean you want an annulment?" Dev asked incredulously. "What kind of fantastical statement is that?"

"It is the truth, Devereaux. I have given this a great deal of thought and have decided that I will no longer hold you to the wager."

"But I don't want an annulment."

"Yes you do," Jena argued.

"Don't tell me what I want, madam!" Dev shouted out of frustration.

Why was he acting so idiotic when she was trying her best to be reasonable? No gentleman would argue with a lady. Ah, she though, understanding at last. "You obviously feel bound by your gentlemanly duty, but that is no longer necessary. I do not expect you to make an honest woman of me, Dev. I want to be free of this marriage as much as you do."

"I will not hear of it," Dev continued as though she had not spoken. "You have won the wager, and that is an end to it."

"You are the stupidest man alive," Jena snapped, her patience at an end. "Please listen carefully to my words. You are no longer bound by the wager.

I do not want to be married to you! I will not stay married to you! I want an annulment!"

"Well, you certainly cannot have one," Dev said, biting off each word precisely. "I refuse to give you one."

Even in the darkness of the garden, Jena could see the stubborn expression plastered on Dev's face. For once she gave in to the urge and drawing her foot back, she kicked him in the shin as hard as she could. At his yelp of pain, she whirled on her heel and raced back through the garden to the safety of the house. She wove her way through the bevy of servants cleaning up after the party and ran along the hallway to the drawing room. She waved at the footmen who threw open the doors for her entry. As the doors closed behind her, she flounced down onto the sofa, her breath coming in ragged gasps. No sooner had she gotten control of her breathing when the doors crashed open and Dev limped into the room.

"There was no need for violence, madam." His tone was one of aggrieved dignity.

"There was every need," Jena snapped. "You are stubborn, pigheaded, arrogant, and . . . and . . ."

"Perverse?" Dev offered. "Obstinate? Stiff-necked? Toplofty?"

"I think I prefer perverse." Despite her best efforts, a smile tugged at the corner of her mouth. "Thank you for the helpful list of words. I will try to remember them," she added primly.

"Now, perhaps we might conduct this conversation with some semblance of decorum. After all, we are both reasonable human beings," Dev finished archly.

"Hah!" she snorted.

Dev could not believe this sudden turn of events. He pushed his hands up through his shaggy white

hair, then brought them down to massage the stiffness from his shoulders and neck. All evening he
had felt his emotions being torn apart. He had arrived for the ball nervous that the evening would
be a disaster and elated that at last the wager
would be at an end. And when Jena had descended
the staircase, her beauty stunned him, filling him
with pride and tenderness and love. He had wanted
to lay the world at her feet. He would have given
her anything he possessed.

Except his trust.

Trust. The word echoed inside Dev's mind, despite his efforts to silence it. All night long Jena
had used the word, and each time it had sent him
into an agony of guilt. He had not placed his trust
in Jena. He had refused to tell her his true feelings
because he was afraid that she would gain control
over him in the same way that his mother had controlled his father. Looking at her, Dev could not
believe that he had ever doubted her. He should
have seen that Jena had a depth to her character
and a fineness of spirit that his mother had not possessed. Jena would never use his love to bludgeon
him with. She might not reciprocate his love, but
she would never turn it against him.

Dev was beginning to realize that unless he could
trust her, he would never be able to establish the
kind of relationship he desired. How could he expect her to love him when he was unwilling to tell
her the truth of his own feelings? It did not matter
whether she could ever love him; he owed her his
trust. Only if he was truly honest with Jena did he
have any hope of winning her love.

Resolutely, Dev squared his shoulders and then
crossed the room to sit down beside Jena. Her eyes
flew open in alarm and she gathered her skirts

around her and moved to the end of the sofa, putting as much distance as she could between them.

"You needn't worry, my dear," Dev drawled. "I do not seek revenge for your unladylike behavior in the garden."

"*My* behavior!" Jena spluttered. "Why, you—"

Dev raised a hand to silence her. "No need to apologize. I have already forgiven you, even though I may be crippled for life."

Jena narrowed her eyes at Dev. She did not understand his sudden change of attitude. He had glowered at her most of the evening, insulted her on the dance floor, and in the garden he had assaulted her like a man possessed. There was an air of playful excitement about him that she did not trust. Before she could think of a caustic retort, Dev began speaking again.

"Perhaps you think we would not suit, Jena." Dev turned toward her, shifting on the sofa so that only one cushion separated him from his wife. "It is true that in the beginning we did not exactly see eye to eye. But over these last months, I thought we were beginning to establish a truce in our relationship. Would you say that was a fair assessment?"

"Y-yes," Jena admitted hesitantly. She looked into Dev's clear blue eyes, but her own dropped before his unswerving glance. She did not know why she felt so uneasy at his questioning. No doubt she was tired after the excitement of the evening and her own emotional turmoil.

Once more Dev changed position, and Jena noticed that now there was only half a cushion separating them. A flutter of panic sent her pulses leaping. She feared his nearness but found she had no power to move.

"I have enjoyed our outings," Dev said. He picked

up Jena's hand that lay limply on her red skirt. He stared down at her fingers and stroked the back of her hand in a gentle rhythm, almost as if he were unconscious of the motion. "I thought we had come a long way to becoming friends. I could be wrong, of course. Mayhap you found my company boring?"

Jena's nerves jangled wildly at his nearness. She found it difficult to form a sentence because her whole attention was focused on the soft stroking motions on the back of her hand. Licking her suddenly dry lips, she croaked, "No. I was not bored."

"I'm glad."

Dev eased closer and now he was beside her. His one arm rested behind her along the back of the sofa. She wanted to move away, but she was trapped in the corner. He still had possession of her hand, but now the stroking motions had progressed to her arm. Jena had trouble keeping her breathing steady for the pounding of her heart. She swallowed with difficulty. Turning her head to speak, she jerked backward at the close proximity of Dev's face. He was smiling, and she found she could not stop staring at his lips.

"We have had an unusual marriage so far." Dev continued as if there had been no break in the conversation. "Although this has been a marriage in name only, I have found that you do not find me totally repulsive."

The arm on the back of the sofa moved to cup Jena's shoulder, and a shiver of anticipation raced through her body. She tried to swallow but this time found her throat constricted. Dev toyed with the sleeve of her dress until it slipped off her shoulder and his fingers smoothed circles on her bare skin. Jena jumped at the contact, sucking in air as though she had been burned. The stroking of his hands had a mesmerizing quality, and a lovely lethargy invaded her body. She sagged against his chest, suspended, waiting for his kiss.

Suddenly the drawing room doors crashed open. Dev leaped to his feet, swearing volubly. It was several seconds before Jena could pull her thoughts back from the spell of eroticism weaving through her head. She blinked her eyes rapidly as the butler appeared in the doorway.

"Good God, Lamb! What is it?" Dev shouted in exasperation at the interruption.

"Do you require anything else this evening, milord?" the butler rasped impassively. Although the pirate wig, hat, and eye patch had been abandoned, it seemed as though the man had forgotten, or more likely, could not bear to part with, the broad-bladed knife.

"No! I mean, yes." Dev took a deep, steadying breath, then continued, "Brandy. And two snifters."

"Very good, your lordship."

Lamb backed out of the room and the doors silently closed. Dev glared at the oak panels, then his glance shifted automatically to the ormolu clock on the mantel. He paced the room, mumbling under his breath and kicking out at the furniture in his path.

Even Jena was flustered by the interruption. She wondered what would have happened if Dev had kissed her. Would it have been different than the passionate embrace in the garden? Dev's whole attitude seemed changed from the glowering man he had been earlier in the evening. He was angry, but at least his fury was directed at Lamb. Looking at him, Jena had to smile at the furtive way he glanced at the clock, awaiting the butler's return.

Finally Dev moved to the fireplace. He rested his shoulders against the mantel, looking totally at his ease, but his unblinking eyes were intent on the closed doors. When they opened with the usual dramatic flourish, he did not react except to narrow his eyes.

"The table will be fine, Lamb."

Dev's eyes followed the man's movements as he set the tray with the decanter and glasses in front of Jena. He waited to speak until the butler was once more framed in the doorway, prepared to back out of the room.

"By the way, Lamb," Dev said. "Please extend our thanks to the entire staff for their assistance tonight. I think it might be appropriate if you could locate some liquid refreshments in the cellar with which they might toast the success of the evening."

"Very good, milord," the butler said. For once the rasping whisper held an approving note. "Will there by anything else, sir?"

"Yes, Lamb. Just a minor point." Dev rubbed his chin reflectively. "Although I will admit that the knife you are wearing must be extremely handy, I fear it sets much too ominous a tone for the casual visitor. Society ladies are decidedly delicate and might be thrown into spasms upon seeing such a grisly object. Perhaps a sword would be more in keeping with your livery," he suggested.

Lamb's expression darkened, to give him, if possible, an even more threatening look than usual. His sausage-shaped fingers fondled the sleek handle of the knife, and his eyes took on a faraway look. Suddenly his face cleared and he surveyed Dev with eyes like slits. "Would your lordship object to a spear?"

"Ah," Dev said, attempting to control the laughter that threatened to undo him. He heard a quickly smothered choking sound issuing from Jena's direction. He did not dare look at her for fear of disgracing himself at the unholy glee he knew he would find in her eyes. The thought of Lamb in his bright yellow livery with a native spear in one hand, and in his other, perhaps a shrunken head, was enough to send the most stalwart into convulsions. With a fine show of enthusiasm, Dev said, "A spear would be just the ticket."

"Very good, your lordship."

The butler sighed in resignation, unspoken criticism of the peculiar vagaries of his master written clearly on his granite face. Then he drew himself to attention, once more preparing to quit the room. The doors began their silent closure only to jerk to a stop at Dev's bark of command.

"One moment, Lamb." Dev cleared his throat, and when he spoke, his voice held only a pleasant conversational one. "There is one small item that I think you could take care of for me."

"Yes, milord?"

"I have come to the realization that her ladyship is of an easily excitable temperament." Dev ignored the gasp of outrage from Jena and continued blandly. "Although I can only applaud the smooth running of the household, it seems that in one area we might improve matters so that my wife will not be sent into fits by the constant jarring of her sensitive nerves. Therefore, in the future I trust you will instruct the footmen on the silent opening and closing of doors, with particular emphasis paid to the doors of this room." Although Dev's voice was still quiet, each word was uttered with great precision. "In other words, Lamb, the next time the doors are flung open in the usual manner, I will personally break both your legs. Is that quite clear?"

"Quite, milord."

Lamb's eyes studied Dev for a moment in silence.

Then his impassive face broke into a wide grin and he snapped his fingers to signal the footmen. In slow motion, the doors glided silently closed.

Dev turned to Jena, and the sight of her desperately fighting to control her amusement made him lose what control he had managed to maintain. He threw back his head, expelling a great shout of laughter. At that, Jena lost her battle and followed suit. It was several minutes before they could return to a more sober attitude.

"You have ruined his game, you know," Jena remarked, wiping her streaming eyes.

Dev crossed the room and grasped the decanter by its neck. He splashed brandy into the snifters and lifted one to present it to Jena.

"I have no doubt, my dear, that Lamb will find some other perfectly odious method of disturbing my peace." Dev stared glumly down at the dark liquid in his glass. "At least the man did not suggest a pike. I would always imagine he had plans for my head."

"Lamb is really quite shy," Jena defended. "You're just afraid to admit that you've grown to like the man."

"Yes, I suppose I have," Dev grumbled. "I still have the vague feeling that one day the Runners will surround the house and haul the entire staff away. But in the meantime, I will have to make the best of things. I've grown used to the whole scurvy lot."

Dev took a sip of the brandy, glancing at Jena over the rim of his glass. He wondered if he would ever get tired of looking at her. She had stripped off her long gloves, and her slender fingers stroked the sides of the cut-glass snifter in her hands. Her head was bent and the silk stream of her hair tumbled across her shoulder. The shimmering mass took on an inky depth against the red of her dress, both color extremes emphasizing the creamy perfection of her skin. Dev ached with the need to touch her but held himself in check.

Lamb's intrusion had come at the worst possible moment. He had managed to establish a wonderful atmosphere for wooing his wife, and the entire scene had been shattered by that idiot's arrival. He suspected that she would be wary of any approach at this point. He did not really know how to proceed.

"Drink your brandy, Jena," Dev said tiredly. "We need to talk over this nonsense."

"It is not nonsense," she said. Beneath his baleful glance, she took a small sip of the potent liquor, then replaced the glass on the table. "I want to forfeit the wager, Dev."

"I've never heard such rubbish. You have won the wager fair and square. You cannot go back on your word. It would not be honorable," he concluded.

Jena stared across at Dev, who had flung himself into an easy chair. His face was set stubbornly, but there was a curious look of bewilderment in his eyes. She wondered why he did not leap at the opportunity she was presenting. He had wanted to be free of the marriage, and yet now he acted as though the idea was outrageous. Would she ever understand the man?

"Why are you being so obstinate?" she asked out of her own confusion.

"Because I must," Dev said, rising from his chair and pacing across to the fireplace. Then he swung around and paced back until he stood directly in front of Jena. "You see, my love, I have made an absolute muddle of everything."

Jena's eyes opened wide at the sound of Dev's

voice. There was such a wealth of emotion in the rich timbre that her pulse began to race even as her mind whirled with the meaning of the endearment he had used. Without thought she rose from the sofa, but before she could make a move, Dev was beside her, taking her hands in his and pulling her against his chest. In wonder she stared up into his face.

"I love you, Jena," he said. "I cannot give you an annulment because I cannot bear for you to leave me. I want you beside me. I need you."

"No, no," Jena cried, terrified to believe his words. "That can't be true."

"But it is, my dear." Dev released her hands, only to reach up and stroke the curve of her cheek. "I don't know how or when it happened, but I love you with my whole heart."

"Are you sure, Dev?" Jena asked. "You have been so adamant about the annulment. I don't know what to believe."

He searched her expression, hoping to find some sign that she returned his feelings, but he could see nothing except puzzlement on her face and a wariness in the stiffness of her body. For a moment his optimism faltered. Had he ruined his chances to win her through his stupidity?

"I know you have no reason to trust me." Dev spoke softly, but there was a vibrancy to his voice that was compelling. "In the beginning I did everything I could to get out of the marriage. I did not want to be married. I felt trapped. Then suddenly I realized that I liked being with you. I enjoyed your conversation, but I also enjoyed the quiet evenings when we read or played a game of chess. Little by little I came to understand that my life was incomplete when you were not a part of it. I want you with me always, Jena."

"You told me you wanted me for your mistress," she accused. "That is passion, not love."

"Passion is part of love, my darling girl." Dev chuckled lecherously and his eyes blazed down at the blushing Jena. "And I will be more than happy to demonstrate that for you."

"Please don't," Jena said in a very small voice.

"For now I will agree to your wishes, but be warned, my dear, when we continue this marriage, it will not be in name only."

Jena pushed away from him, moving across the room to stare blindly out of the windows overlooking the darkened garden. Her eyes were filled with tears as the wonder of Dev's words finally pierced her mind. She had wanted his love, and now that she had it, her heart felt as though it might burst with joy.

"I did not mean to frighten you, Jena," Dev said, misunderstanding her agitation. "I realize that this sudden turnaround must be bewildering. It must be difficult for you to forgive much of what I have said and done. But I love you and I think that, given time, you might come to love me, too. I will woo you slowly as I should have done if we had met in some other way. Please do not feel that I will rush you. I would never force my attentions on you."

Jena's back remained stubbornly turned, and Dev waited in agony for a sign she might be willing to forgive him and begin anew. Finally she spoke, her voice just above a whisper.

"I wouldn't mind if you forced your attentions on me."

"What?"

"I said, you great gudgeon, I wouldn't mind."

Dev leaped across the room, grabbed Jena's shoulders, and whirled her around to face him. Her head was bent and he could see the flush of color that rose from the neckline of her dress. His heart began to race wildly in his chest as he reached out to lift her chin. He sucked in his breath at the warmth in Jena's gray eyes.

"Oh, Jena, is it possible you have some feeling for me?" he asked hesitantly.

"I fell in love with you ages ago. Why do you think I wanted the annulment?" Jena did not wait for his answer, wanting to tell him everything. "You told me you would acknowledge the marriage in order to save my name and reputation. No matter how much I wanted your love, I knew that would be a disaster. I was so afraid you would grow to hate me if you felt the marriage had been forced on you."

"I have been awful, my darling." Dev kissed her forehead and her eyelids.

"You were hateful," Jena said. "Especially the morning after the wedding."

"I was furious with you. I thought you were an actress trying to profit from the drunken idiocy of my actions." He nuzzled her ear and then dipped lower to kiss the side of her neck.

"And then you forced me into that dreadful wager."

Jena was having difficulty concentrating as Dev's mouth roamed up along her neck to her cheek. He stopped at the corner of her mouth and she waited, her body tensed with anticipation. He did not disappoint her. His kiss this time was infinitely tender. There was passion aplenty, but his touch was light, asking for a response, not wresting it from her. Jena opened to him, love wrapping around them and holding them close.

"I have a great deal to apologize for," Dev said as he raised his head. He reached up to her hair, searching for the pins that held her braid in place.

Finding them, he hurled them impatiently to the floor, returning for the rest. His fingers unwound the plaits, combing through the silken mass until it tumbled freely down her back. "I have wanted to do that since the first morning in the library."

"You hated me then," Jena said.

"I desired you," Dev said, holding up his hand when she would have interrupted. "Perhaps I loved you even then. All I knew was that I was obsessed by an infuriating, outrageous, scheming baggage. Your gray eyes haunted my daydreams. My desire for you kept me awake at night. You are a witch. A siren. A vixen." Dev punctuated each word with a kiss. Suddenly he threw his head back in a great shout of laughter. He cupped her face in his hands, smiling down at the astonishment on Jena's face. "What could be more appropriate, my darling love. A vixen for the Gray Fox."